The Sick List

The Sick List

by Ansgar Allen

Beyond Criticism Editions

BOILER HOUSE PRESS

Each book we produce testifies to the intellectual death of its author, as Gordon would say. Not worth reading and hardly read, he said, the intellect crawls into them and dies. It is no accident that books of this sort are placed beyond the grasp of so-called ordinary people. Ordinary people, as Gordon might say, must not discover that the university—the place of thought—is the death of thought. Even academics avoid the books they produce. They produce these books, call them *monographs*, and barely ever read them. The secret of these books, about them being the graveyard of the intellect, he continued, remains well guarded. They remain closed, mostly, and if opened are not much read. Most books are merely owned. The impulse to write a book for those moved to do so, *for those sick enough for the writing of them*, is considerable. These books are not recognised as the graveyard of the intellect because the intellect that reads them has already perished. A diminished readership long afflicted by the death of thought cannot see the intellectual catastrophe that is written into its books, he said. The compulsion to write survives, aided by the fact none recognise them as such, as monuments to dead or decaying intellect. Although most who suffer from this sickness fail to write the books they are sick enough to read, they spend their time wishing they were writing them, mourning those books they've not yet written. They grieve for these unwritten books as if they were written but lost, and pass their time writing academic papers, or hoping to write papers, in which, as Gordon would say, the situation is much worse. Gordon had more restraint than most, I thought. He was immune to the writing of books. Gordon was even immune to the thought of writing them when not writing them. Even his thought about the university as a graveyard of the intellect could not prompt Gordon to write. Gordon knew, I felt, as with most ideas hatched whilst walking to and from work, that this idea would not endure the kind of scrutiny his profession expected. Gordon's office was a place where thinking was impossible. It is impossible to think at work, in the university, Gordon would say. Its offices are not places of thought. At its best, the university office was a place one might sit and ponder the deplorable state of the world. Now even that thinking about the deplorable state of things is ruled out, and as such, the university has no further function. Thinking is purged from working life. Thoughts like this one about thinking at work are purged. Thoughts about the university and thoughts about the book sickness are also purged. For my profession, thoughts in themselves and thoughts about thoughts must be worked up at work and transformed into print, or they must remain quiet as thoughts not worth publishing. Either way they are purged. We exchanged ideas by resorting to print. The irony did not escape me. Gordon's thought was conveyed through what Gordon was reading or had once read, so I thought, where Gordon generally avoided *monographs* and had a way of mis-reading what he failed to avoid. I would discover what Gordon was reading because Gordon walked with a book under his arm. If I caught sight of the title, I read it myself. Gordon's books were often from the library, allowing me to read the exact copy I had seen Gordon holding days before. Gordon's book-carrying habit was accompanied by a pen-carrying habit. The two habits were connected. Gripped tightly in Gordon's fist as he walked was a piston-fill pen. I never saw Gordon without it. His hands were stained with green ink from constant refilling. His pen was operated by drawing ink through a nib that would subsequently bleed. It covered Gordon's fingers as he withdrew it from the inkpot and blotted it dry. That pot may very well be on his person, I thought, to make the constant refilling of the pen more convenient to a man clearly in need of ink. His fingers would not become that stained from merely writing with the pen, I thought. The persistent ink stain that I observed without fail, unless I failed to see, had to be from constant refilling. Gordon most probably travelled with a pot of ink. Obviously, Gordon had to refill in a range of situations, some less convenient than others. Gordon frequently had nothing to blot with but his fingers. Though Gordon was not a writer, or not anymore, Gordon did underline, highlight, and occasionally annotate. The evidence was abundant. It accounted for the ink. Gordon trailed green ink across the books he read. Gordon filled books with marks, dashes, encirclements, and the odd comment. The first book I read under Gordon's influence drained his pen more than most. It was a respectable book on a crude topic, a chronicle of farts and related outbursts in medieval texts. After Gordon checked it back into the library, I checked it out, extracting sentences Gordon underlined in green. I read these passages as if they were highlighted for my benefit. Gordon left traces quite deliberately for me (or someone like me) to pick up, I decided. I coped with the task of reading Gordon's books by telling myself his notations were for me, or someone similar, so that it might just as well be me. Given the undeniable fact that this book was written by my namesake, it had to be an invitation from Gordon to me, I told myself, or gave myself permission to think. These traces were for my personal edification. It was necessary to come to that conclusion, actually, to cope with the tedium of reading Gordon's books. Regarding this particular one, it was reasonable to assume Gordon wished me to begin with it. I would commence my study under Gordon precisely here with this book annotated by Gordon. Gordon would begin talking about that book by telling me he admired the word drutling. Every time the word *drutling* was used, Gordon underlined it twice, the first time with an asterisk. It is a scholarly book he would have said, I thought. It diligently footnotes each scatological record, for *the book does not call for abandonment of the rules of academic engagement.* There is, nonetheless, *much affectionate parodying of them.* That annotation appeared just inside the front cover. It was a quote from comments made elsewhere, written by the author of this book on farting.[1] When speaking I imagined Gordon would give the reference in a similar way, appended as a footnote to our conversation. Footnote, he would say. As a result of this tendency to footnote, our speech developed a mechanical inflection. It was punctured by the mechanics of continually referencing what we said, perforated by references, page numbers and publication details. Everything we said was footnoted where appropriate. It was the death of thought all this footnoting, I thought, as Gordon would say. We have long fallen ill of this endless need for references and page numbers, they serve as our intellectual props. That is why we could tolerate this book, another monograph filled with footnotes and references. On my estimation, Gordon went on, this book does not subvert what it parodies. This book manifests (Gordon indicated in the margin) the academic ideal that science in the broadest sense (*Wissenschaft*) should be pursued for its own sake and the university should be left to its own devices. Despite its scatological title, Gordon said, as I listened, and despite some of its contents, this book sits comfortably within academic convention. Decrepit yes. Decidedly weak as it may have become, this lapsed university tradition still believes it is better off left alone. Leave us alone, it demands.

---

1   Valerie, Allen. Author's Response to Professor Danuta Shanzer, review of *On Farting: Language and Laughter in the Middle Ages*, (review no. 733). *Reviews in History* 2009.

Contributions to knowledge should not be reduced to an estimation of their use-value, as an academic might put it, because that would be mere commerce. This chronicle of the medieval fart maintains its distance from worldly things in a similar way. It makes itself useless by picking a point-less topic. And in its form too, the style of the book resists summation by embracing the disorder of its subject matter, he said. It declares, though not in so many words, *leave us alone and let the university be*. Gordon changed tack. His writing had run thin. There were several attempts to under-line and further annotate that delivered little ink to the page. Gordon pressed harder and scratched about, attempt-ing to underscore text. I feared for the nib. All this scratch-ing became random, wrought backwards and forwards as if Gordon would rather scratch about and wear the page thin than fill his pen. He was always running out of ink and fill-ing up. So much I already knew. Gordon left a trail of ink and because he left that trail, he was always running out of it. He filled books with so much green ink his pen was con-stantly running empty. This running out of ink was insuffer-able for someone like Gordon, I supposed. It was a nuisance that made Gordon scratch about for some considerable time before finally relenting and refilling his pen. All that scratching was followed by a blot. Gordon had relented and refilled his piston-pen. Parts of the introduction after that excursus of scratching, filling and blotting were heavily underlined, ruined. This book, Gordon underlined, *offers no reduction of thought and only lengthens the task of reading*. It does not seek to contribute to thought as if it could only expel thought. Concerned with the matter of waste, it includes within its catalogue not only bodily waste, but also *scientifically obsolete bodies of knowledge* of which there could be no better repository than the Middle Ages, *itself the waste lot of redundant knowledge and "false" etymologies... The Middle Ages*, it continues, Gordon underlined, and I quote, *provides a vantage point from which to rethink modernity's preoccupation with accumulation.*[2] We might think of this book as *drutling*, we are told, Gordon noted—and this is what attracted me (him)—it describes the activity of a dog or horse that *frequently stops in its way, and ejects a small quantity of dung at intervals.*[3] It farts around. Its progress is non-teleological. I liked it for that, Gordon said, so I decided. The book models itself on *the fart* or *the bum*. It claims to take seriously the idea that the formless fart could mirror itself in the *formless book*, a book that only the arse would produce, not the mouth or the fingers.[4] But the modern research scholar is not writing from the arse, or bum, Gordon mused (I assumed), and this author is no exception. Gordon had written *no bum*, under the author's name on the title page, and again *no bum* at repeated intervals seemingly at random throughout the book. The book had been filled by the words *no bum*. Actually, much of what I deduce about Gordon reads backwards from this notation. It occurred so often and with such force in that sickly green ink of Gordon's that the phrase no bum came to occupy my

2   Allen, Valerie. *On Farting: Language and Laughter in the Middle Ages*. Basingstoke: Palgrave Macmillan, 2010. p. 1.

3   Allen. *On Farting*. p. 1.

4   Allen. *On Farting*. p. 6.

mind more than any other. The words no bum entirely over-came all words printed in the book. It was all *no bum*. I nod-ded. Had Gordon noticed my reaction, my emphatic nod-ding in response to the repeated refrain, *no bum*, I suspect he would have abandoned me. It was too assured, too much of an argument, this statement. It was also the longest piece of analysis Gordon ever allowed me to assemble with assur-ance. These notations were the closest Gordon approached sustained argument. Having reached the end of our path, we parted ways. I think it was fortunate we met like that, that day, and days since, though I am not entirely convinced if it was my good fortune or not to meet Gordon, given that, from a different view, it was entirely to my detriment. Parts of me would like to dismiss Gordon entirely. Actually, as soon as I met Gordon I wanted to be rid of him. In his com-pany I felt uneasy. My role in our relationship, or not-rela-tionship, was never clear. Gordon held my attention as he travelled from work, though he did so very little to maintain it. I could not decide if Gordon was teaching me directly by the clues he left, or if he worked to deceive me by the very same clues, in which case everything I thought subsequent to Gordon would be the product of that deception. Surely, I thought, that would be the task of *the last educator*. We both shared the intuition, so I felt, that education must end. The end of education was approaching, and must approach, it was inevitable that education must end. We were ending it. Gordon and I and the rest of our profession were supervis-ing, inaugurating the end of education, the end of an attach-ment. Education has reached the final, most disordered phase of its development. In it, by way of it, we represent the last configuration of habits and habitual beliefs that can still culminate in the impression of a thing, an entity, and a belief in that entity, even though it is a non-entity, a rolling disaster, a so-called good that everyone values but nobody can revive, *and so it must end*, I thought, though not before exhausting itself grotesquely. Gordon indicated to me he had no idea what education stood for, and that if education stood for anything it most likely stood for nothing and had been in that condition of standing for nothing for some considerable time. *I would wipe my arse on education*, Gordon would say, *if there were anything educational at hand to do the wiping with*. Given a little time and space to fill out the details Gordon could lecture on that topic, write a paper on it, perhaps even pull together a book about education, an *educational* book in the worst and true sense, and then use that book to wipe his arse with. But Gordon had no compulsion to write. This thought like every other thought I associated with Gordon would not warrant a book by Gordon, scarcely even a paper or lecture. He would never wipe his arse on a book like that. The last educator would never write a book about the end of education, unless that book was a monstrous distortion. The last educator would not teach, at least not directly. Though Gordon would never accept such a grandiose term, *the last educator*, the educator who teaches the last lesson before the end of education, would be someone like him. Emerging from some corridor, or passage, a dead end most probably, the last educator would offer a lesson of complete and utter deception, a lesson in deceit that would be announced as such. Dissimulation, suspicion, confusion, and finally, darkness. That was Gordon's art, I thought, closing the *monograph*. Besides which Gordon preferred another book, I decided, since he walked with it for longer, which is to say more than just once, if not repeatedly, and held it more closely, walking with *History of Shit* under his arm. The book Gordon now held was written by a Frenchman who died young.[5] Holding Gordon to be my educator, adopting Gordon as a kind of private tutor, and believing that he sought to aggravate me—for that is how I understood educational relationships—it struck me as no coincidence that Gordon was holding this book by an author who was precisely my age when he died. Or, if it was a coincidence, I continued to think, it was one for me to ponder. The fact that if I had been him, or, if he had been me, I or he, with him now being me would be dead now or nearly dead, seemed important. This discussion, which was really a discussion about nothing, took us to the end of our path. Gordon's copy was not from the library nor was it in the library, so I bought one of my own. On the day of my purchase, with *History of Shit* in my bag, a colleague who was retiring spoke to me about Gordon. The occasion of his retirement caused him to stray beyond the usual office chit-chat. He confided in me that he too had known Gordon on the very same path I now took, and that by some strange coincidence Gordon had been reading Laporte's *History of Shit* then too. That was some time ago. Gordon once spoke quite a bit, or at least listened, and by listening encouraged others to speak. For my part, when Gordon was silent, I was

---

5   Laporte, Dominique. *History of Shit*. Cambridge, Massachusetts: MIT Press, 2002 [1978].

silent, it makes little sense to speak to someone who might not listen. And given that Gordon had never spoken, at least not to me, I had never uttered a word in reply. Like most people I know, the retiree did not suffer in that way. When confronted by silence, he filled it with noise. I sat before him giving all outward signs of disinterest, as was my habit. He responded as expected. Overly talkative, as if knowing he was about to be forgotten by the institution that once employed him, the man struggled against his growing irrelevance by dredging up memories of Gordon. Reeking of retirement already (the institution would never be irrelevant to him), he told me how he'd once told Gordon about someone he'd known who'd enjoyed pointing out to himself (and all who would listen) the *shit-pipes* on the exterior walls of older buildings. Our world is built upon channelled and culverted flows of shit, my predecessor told Gordon, he told me. It struck me that his thoughts had become grandiose, too inflated for Gordon's tastes. *Tell your acquaintance to read Laporte* was all Gordon said, he told me. I could feel Gordon's irritation, I thought. Gordon was irritated, I decided, because my predecessor's acquaintance was already too serious to learn much from the channels of muck he so admired. You cannot learn about all this shit with such seriousness, I thought. Those shit-pipes and all that muck simply won't edify you if you approach it like that. Overly serious people do not have the capacity to learn much at all from all the filth we produce and distribute across the face of the earth. And that is the lesson of *History of Shit*, I decided. That book lacks seriousness concerning the subject of shit precisely when it should, I thought. But my predecessor could only tell me about what Gordon said in relation to that book, which was not, in truth, very much at all. What Gordon said to my predecessor told him almost nothing about the book and very little about Gordon. *Tell your acquaintance to read Laporte*, Gordon said, my predecessor told me. My predecessor told me that twice, quoting Gordon quite precisely so he said. But there is only so much you can make of that statement, to *tell your acquaintance to read Laporte*. You could repeat it, as my predecessor had already done several times, but eventually you run out of things to say about a statement like that. So, my predecessor spent most of the time he occupied talking to me about Gordon telling me what Gordon *did not say*. Since Gordon did not say rather a lot, my predecessor was prone to speculate about Gordon. He told me at length about what Gordon *did not say* but might have said had he spoken. My predecessor was reduced to such an impoverished level of conjecture built so thin and on so little evidence that I found his conversation almost completely unbearable. I found him unbearable. His knowledge of Gordon was extremely speculative. It was almost pointless, I thought, and deserved all the outward signs of disinterest I was able to give him but which he was entirely ill-equipped to decipher. Our conversation or not-conversation was almost nearly pointless, I decided. The more he spoke about Gordon, the less he demonstrated knowledge of Gordon. His talking about Gordon was almost completely senseless, and so unbearable. His Gordon was clearly a figment of his (impoverished) imagination. My predecessor was entirely deluded in thinking that he knew Gordon, I thought. I only indulged him because we were celebrating his retirement, or so I said to myself, and my indulgence, which was really a non-indulgence, was already more than he deserved. I sat there looking at him talking to me about Gordon, thinking to myself, if you were not retiring I would not tolerate you telling me about Gordon. He rambled on with such minimal indulgence on my part because of his retirement do. In any other situation I would not have tolerated his talking to me about Gordon at all. It is customary to be generous and not a little stupid with respect or what goes for respect at a retirement do, and so I listened with growing irritation to his complete and utter distortion of Gordon. Everything he said about Gordon was a falsification of Gordon. I would only suffer his endless speculation about Gordon because he was retiring. As he told me about Gordon, going on about Gordon as he did, and as I listened to him talking about Gordon, looking at this man who was telling me about Gordon even though I did not want to listen to him telling me about Gordon since *his* Gordon was a complete distortion, I thought that it was just about bearable his speaking to me because tomorrow he would be retired, which is like death in the academy. I looked into his eyes and thought: tomorrow you will be retired. My predecessor was about to be retired, I told myself, and so I could bear his talking to me about Gordon, about a man he did not know, but thought he knew, a combination of self-assurance and ignorance I found utterly sickening. He told me so much about what Gordon *did not say* that I became increasingly convinced Gordon had barely ever spoken to him, if at all. He added that he remembered this exchange quite precisely, right down to the smallest detail. He remembered quite precisely how Gordon had said *tell your friend to read Laporte.* Or was it, *tell your acquaintance to read Laporte?* I could not be bothered to ask. That addition, about the smallest detail, only furthered my irritation. You are retiring, I told myself again. I looked into his eyes as he spoke to me, I looked right into his eyes, and told myself: *you are retiring.* If you were not about to retire, I would not tolerate you telling me all this about Gordon. That last thing he said about remembering right down to the smallest detail actually enraged me. I was convinced by that addition, about remembering quite precisely what Gordon had said, that his rendition of Gordon and what Gordon did not say but said nonetheless, was a hateful rendition and was nothing but a distortion of the most mendacious sort. My predecessor was notoriously untrustworthy and would over-state himself as dependable in an attempt to counteract his bad reputation. When he finally finished talking to me about Gordon, and went to speak to another, I just turned and walked away. I walked away from this man, my predecessor, and that was that. Tomorrow you will be retired, I told myself walking away. I tolerated you because you were retiring, I said to myself. And completely ignoring everything he had said to me about Gordon, I turned in subsequent days to Laporte's *History of Shit*. My predecessor had never read that book, I thought. It was not in the library, had never been requested, and surely had not been privately purchased by my predecessor. He was well known for never buying books. My predecessor lived entirely without books. His office was almost completely empty of books apart from a small pile he borrowed at intervals from the library. But even that borrowing habit eventually stopped. Which hardly made a difference since he avoided that small pile of library books. It just sat there like most library books do, stacked up, unread, and waiting to be returned. My predecessor prided himself on not reading. I have read enough, he would say. I have spent most of my life reading and do not need to read any more. It's all up there, he frequently said, tapping his head. As he tapped his head, he tapped not books but everything else that is stuffed into the human skull besides books. He tapped his head and nothing happened. It was unusual back then for him to say these things. Now it's not at all unusual to spend weeks at work without opening a book. Then it was strange to find oneself not opening a book at work every day, or at least every other day, or once a week, if only to put it aside. Now the reading of books at work is avoided, and the holding of books looks odd. It reeks of inactivity. If reading happens at all it must happen quickly. If you open a book elsewhere, in the library or on the bus, you find yourself only scanning the pages of the book in your hands, wondering about something else because you have forgotten how to read. And you tell yourself that you are reading, but in truth you are only scanning, you think all reading is scanning because you have forgotten how to read, and if you finally remember that reading is not always scanning it becomes apparent that you have become temperamentally opposed to reading, so you fill yourself with coffee and sit back down, but you have become skittish, and tell yourself I will return to reading with a finger and relearn the art of connecting words, I will sit here until I learn to read again, I will force myself to read each word before me at an even pace, I am about to read every word on this page, you determine, as you admonish yourself for every word you skip, and say, I will no longer skip even a single paragraph, I will no longer glance through and then skip entire pages, chapters, and whole books, but the reading still fails to gather up words and deposit them in your head, your ability to read has been entirely ruined by reading and will continue to be ruined so long as you read these books. Most books do not deserve to be read line-by-line. Academic books are not to be read in full. To read an academic book from first page to last is to die with that book, I could hear Gordon say. Academia already ruined its ability to read by the time my predecessor announced he no longer read. It lost the ability to distinguish between books worth reading line-by-line, and books that must be scanned and quickly discarded. These books must be abandoned very quickly to avoid the illness books produce in the mind of the reader, which yawns open and petrifies. These books announced the end of thought for their readership before my time. That is why academics no longer think, or when they think, struggle to think anything more than the thought of wanting to think. Not that we ever amounted to much as thinking beings. As thinkers we are entirely over-rated. We occupy most of the time we spend thinking, or attempting to think, overrating ourselves as thinking beings. Most thought is an attempt to exaggerate the extent to which we can think at all. It is true that thinking at work, such as it ever existed, is now more unusual than ever. In today's university the academic mostly avoids thinking, or the pretence of thinking. The academic is preoccupied with the pretence of doing. If the academic thinks, thinking must take the form of doing. For today's academic, thinking without doing is wasted doing. Reading, which might be considered a form of thinking, must be carried out as if it were a form of doing. Reading sitting forward is better than reading sitting back. Reading with a pen, or with a keyboard, is better than reading without. To read at work, openly, is not advisable. Reading gives the impression of thinking without doing. The academic does, and must be seen to be doing, at all times. The academic thinks when commanded to do so, when the job requires it. Produced in such moments, thoughts are strewn about, spread across the working day. Such thoughts may sound connected, but they are linked together and largely drowned out by the sound of doing. In the university today even writing is more doing than thinking. Even less thinking occurs in the writing of books than before, in the production of texts that were never monuments to thought, only the death of thought. The intellect no longer needs to crawl into books to die. Thinking is already splintered by the act of doing. My predecessor only ever did things. And in that respect, he was ahead of his time. He just sat at work doing things or talking about those many things that he would be doing, had to do, had not yet managed to do, and would begin to do again as soon as he finished talking and returned to his desk. When he returned to his desk it was clear that he was not really doing anything at all, but was still thinking about how much he had to do, and would begin doing, soon enough. In that way he cycled between doing things, which was always a way of not doing things, and talking about doing things, the very things he didn't do. He never thought all that much, and certainly never read *History of Shit*. My predecessor was a prototype, I decided. He was retired as a prototype when better models of himself superseded him, people like me. His contemporaries sat about reading and talking about reading. Sometimes they wrote. They even thought a little, in a piecemeal, pedantic kind of way. And when they did things, they often did them. They did not talk endlessly about all the things they had to do, and would continue doing, when they stopped talking. Influenced by that thought, or half-thought of how my predecessors might have thought when reading, I opened the book, trying to read *History of Shit* as they might have done, line-by-line, word-by-word attempting to think a little myself in a diminished kind of way. Things at work were becoming completely unliveable as we are in the habit of saying. The state of the university today is one of near-ruin. Though few would put it in these terms, as Gordon might say, we scarcely have the time to write those awful books we were once known for. The university is so diminished and inhibits thought to such an extent, that it even discourages the writing of such awful, thought-inhibiting books. When they appear, these books are celebrated all the more as achievements against the odds, though these books are only a higher, earlier form of the same catastrophe. In some respects, nothing has changed. Other ways of killing the intellect have simply risen to prominence. One form of intellectual death has been substituted for another. Still, *History of Shit* has to be an outlier, I decided. Three days before I saw Gordon holding that remarkable book, a colleague of his, or at least someone who worked in the same department, was found sitting at his desk suffering from the advanced effects of dehydration. He had not been seen outside his office for three days. Gordon's colleague had been sitting on his swivel chair since Tuesday. On Friday he was discovered. Nothing could be done to revive the colleague from his stupor. He had stopped doing things and talking about the things he had not yet done but needed to do. So when I finally got hold of *History of Shit*, I really did try to read it. *History of Shit* was a useful diversion. Gordon's co-worker was the talk of the institution. We all talked about Gordon's co-worker and the things he would have been doing, and talking about doing, if he had not just stopped doing them. *History of Shit* came at an important time then. I would escape all this talk about Gordon's co-worker by reading that book. The book I distracted myself with opens by quoting an Edict written to ensure all subsequent edicts of the sovereign courts and subaltern or secondary institutions in France were, *clear beyond doubt* and *written with a clarity that will remove all ambiguities or uncertainties which may give rise to subsequent interpretations than the ones intended*. Later in that same year of 1539 a second edict appeared in France, whereby, *François, King of France by the Grace of God, makes known to all present and all to come our displeasure at the considerable deterioration visited upon our good city of Paris and its surroundings, which has so degenerated into ruin and destruction that one cannot journey through it either by carriage or on horseback without meeting with great peril and inconvenience*. The city, it declares, was *filthy and glutted with mud, animal excrement, rubble and other offals. Against all reason*, it continues, city dwellers had seen fit to leave this shit *heaped before their doors*, provoking *great horror and greater displeasure in all valiant persons of substance*. All this corruption and stench was clearly the work of *corrupted individuals* and demanded a hasty and robust response. *Article 4* forbids the emptying and tossing into the streets of the aforementioned muck, demanding it be retained along with all *stagnant and sullied waters and urines inside the confines of your homes* before being carried out of the city.[6] This dramatic opening to the book, Laporte's book, establishes a link then, between the cleansing of language and the cleaning of streets. It seems unlikely that the two were connected, indeed conjoined, as intimately as Laporte suggests, though this connection, and our indebtedness to it, explains quite a bit, I thought. Operating in tandem, the cleansing of language and the cleaning of streets worked to produce the functions and architecture of modern subjectivity. This entire world, our world, the one we are made for, and make in our image, is a thing to do with shit and the cleaning up of shit, I thought, the shit on the streets and the shit in our mouths, although it never succeeded, we testify to that, and by failing, led to redoubled attempts, a digging in, an entrenchment in mire that we shovel from one side of the pit, or mouth, to the other. Laporte's pre-history of shit traces the unmitigated shitness of our contemporary world order back to *the peculiar organization of knowledge that was the Renaissance*. The pith of which, regarding language, was the Renaissance belief that if language is to be made beautiful *it must be because a mas-*

---

6   Laporte. *History of Shit.* pp. 3–4.

ter bathes it—a master who cleans shit holes, sweeps offal, and expurgates city and speech.[7] According to this Renaissance logic, *without a master, one cannot be cleaned.* Whether *by fire or by the word, by baptism or by death*, purification *requires submission to the law.*[8] Language must be washed and policed so that none *need fear pollute his mouth.*[9] What *fattens language without enriching it* must be removed.[10] Scribes once made the task of copyist bearable by embellishment, Laporte claims, adding letters here and there. The printing press eradicated this corruption, which filled up paper with *superfluous orthographies.* For Laporte, however, *that which is expelled inevitably returns.* The expulsion of superfluous orthographies, of pointless letters, would only succeed at the cost of their return in a more regimented, relentless form. Typeset, better organised, letters were only unleashed with greater incontinence with the mass production of books, through the overproduction, the compulsion to authorship which rules academic labour in particular. We have a book writing disease, I thought, or at least a paper writing disease. The printing press suppressed the ridiculous embellishments of the scribe, but the *shit came back.*[11] The press ended up mass-producing the shit it laboured so hard to set in type. Academia is backing up. The pipes are filled with its waste. New journals are inaugurated every year, but we are still running out of places to shove it, I

---

7   Laporte. *History of Shit.* p. 7.
8   Laporte. *History of Shit.* p. 2.
9   Laporte. *History of Shit.* p. 8.
10   Laporte. *History of Shit.* p. 9.
11   Laporte. *History of Shit.* p. 15.

thought, when we should be running out of faith this endless shoving is worth doing in the first place. Faith would disappear, there is ample reason, if it were not for the fact that faith has become habit, just as habit became faith. It is no longer necessary to believe that what we shove is worth producing. If we shove enough, the activity of shoving itself becomes sanctified. But the system in which we invest so much time ends up producing so much excess, useless material, I decided, that we can no longer ignore how much shit we produce. Surrounded by this shit, which is building up everywhere and making us sick, we still operate as if we were producing more than dead material, as if we were forever refining thought, advancing knowledge, defending humanity, and so on. That is our fantasy, the fantasy of an academic above shit, or at least against it, of thinking without producing shit, I thought. But this desire to render things intelligible, to order and systematise, regulate and make calculable, to account for life by any means so long as they obey a method of inspection, *and then publish it*, is forever defeated by the excess it produces. Too many books destroy the intelligibility of things. Too much book reading petrifies the mind that hopes to think. Gordon and I, I decided, and all that surrounded us, were its waste products. When I think about how much I have already read, I feel emptier than I feel I ought. When I think about how much I still hope to read, I feel sick before the thought of it. I tap my head and there is nothing there but an abstract sense of guilt. It should be full of books, or the effects of books. But I tap my head and feel empty of books. With each polluting gesture we testify to their failure to order our existence, render it calculable, give it meaning, dignify and guide it. We tap our heads and there is nothing there by way of books, not even papers. Even the greatest books we have ever read do nothing for us when we need them most. As writers of books and books about books we are becoming superfluous, I thought. Not in self-defence, I decided, as if we hoped to become self-professed, self-cultivated icons of useless erudition—a ridiculous, vacuous idea. The traditional argument for the university insists that intellectual life is best understood as a *system of manners* that we defend as if that system were the mainstay of society, or could become the basis of a better one. Apparently, those who ask what the university is for betray themselves instantly as uncultivated, uninitiated, enslaved to the present, whereas those with good intellectual manners know implicitly but refuse to state the value of their art. Explicit statements regarding the value of academic life are betrayals symptomatic of a base misunderstanding. To go forth and evaluate the value of university life and give it a robust externally assayable defence is to misapprehend the value of intellectual culture. The worth of intellectual culture is as ineffable as it is boundless, where the strongest argument for it, by its own account, amounts to an argument for nothing, I thought. It gestures to a space of possibility and spends the rest of its time filling that space with writing, thought about writing when not writing, and talk about doing when not doing. It argues for the continued support of a realm where nothing can reduce it to anything, and then quickly stuffs that hole with print and talk about print, too much to ever read or endure. It stuffs that space with words, I decided, and we subsequently become sick with them. We are sick with the words we have read and the words we have not yet read. When we think about all the words we have written down we are left empty. They amount to nothing by comparison to their promise. When we think about all the words we have not yet written down, but might still write, we feel sick, or would feel sick if we could entertain the thought of them. Intellectual culture is sick with words, I thought. These words are useless to us. We read them and feel tired by way of them. Then we write more of them, filling a void that we are told, as we tell ourselves, we should not have to defend in terms other than our own ineffable intuition of the importance of intellectual culture. The uselessness of the academy remains its original defence, I thought, even though that argument is instantly betrayed by its history, since the first and highest mission of the medieval university was to manufacture and reproduce a priesthood. It would then produce lawyers, statesmen and doctors, masters in the practical arts of duplicity and control. What haunts the contemporary academic, then, is a growing sense of weakness unfamiliar to the profession. Gordon knew that. The traditional defence—entirely spurious, deceptive—is now accompanied by a second, opposite argument that survives quite well in the corpse of its predecessor. The university declares to all who will listen that it is useful after all. Greed and desperation comingle, a disgusting mix, and the university is finally rendered useless before its own growing systems of obsessive self-inspection. None of which could explain the presence of Gordon in this tired, delusional system. He was differently useless. Gordon was almost completely ineffective as a lecturer, or so I'd heard it whispered, though he was not quite inept. There was no purity to his ineptitude. Gordon was an appalling colleague by all conventional standards. His very existence impeded the efficiency of all who worked in relation to him as he drove them to frustration. For that reason alone, they generally avoided Gordon. His slowness, his refusal to communicate, was legendary. Gordon's obstructive presence was to all practical effects largely ignored, however, since no one confronted Gordon on that account. Gordon was experienced as a vague but deep-set irritant. Even indirect contact via Gordon's students impeded the efficiency of other lecturers and made them sense the basic futility of their work, since those he taught carried the effects of Gordon's teaching and the confusion it inspired to other classes. Hesitant and bewildered students were his speciality. They posed a special problem to the institution, since these students were no longer sure what they were doing there and were no longer secure in their habits. They milled about and wondered quite openly what this place was for. Gordon's students looked at their lecturers as if they had never seen such perversion. They sat, impassive and slack-jawed, looking at those who would teach them, unable to shed the suspicion that the entire university was as pointless before itself as it was before others. Students intuit best what their lecturers deny. Gordon's students carried this basic intuition to excess. Three weeks after Gordon's co-worker was found, dehydrated and still, two more co-workers were discovered in a similar condition. They were both sitting in their respective offices, entirely motionless. One had not been seen since Monday and was discovered on Thursday sitting on his swivel chair facing the computer. The other had not been seen since Tuesday and was discovered on the following Monday. This co-worker had been sitting at her desk for the entire week-end and was again severely dehydrated. They put her straight on a drip. *They put her straight on a drip*, we all repeated, relating to one another this latest sequence of events and remarking at the brutal efficiency of our employ-er which already had drips, a trainee from the Department of Nursing, and all the necessary equipment on standby in anticipation. They would not be caught by surprise a second time. It was tedious to me, all this talk, which was the talk of the institution. My preferred tedium was entirely different, and I retreated to it. Gordon was differently tedious, I reflected. Gordon was a pain of sorts, in the arse, so to speak. Most teachers are. But he wasn't a pain in the arse in any conventional sense. Gordon could not be dismissed for being a pain in the arse, but Gordon approached dismissal. He approached but never quite reached the limits of every-day incompetence. Gordon could not be had by his employ-er for deliberate misconduct. His conduct was perverse but could not be distinguished as such. Operating in a context that is in many respects beyond perversion, Gordon set his fulcrum elsewhere. He found leverage at the limits of pro-fessionalism, at the point where acceptable incompetence approaches punishable misconduct. That was his art. Gor-don's borderline incompetence goaded those who would like to dismiss him, or declare him inept and unlawful, have him sacked or arrested, or even better, rendered inert and removed to some forgotten corner of society. Those who encountered Gordon wanted to ignore him on the basis that he was some kind of social excrescence, a reprobate, or, at the other extreme, on the excuse that his existence was so unremarkable it could barely warrant notice. Gordon would slip from sight either way. You wanted to do this to him. Everything about Gordon invited you to do so but nothing about Gordon allowed your dislike of Gordon to pass over into total disregard. That was his genius. Gordon lingered on and prolonged the will to dismissal in those he encountered so that it became unbearable. Assimilate or dismiss, Gordon made both impossible. It was his art, and his alone so far as I knew. It was the art of unbearable ambiguity. But there is a danger still, and I think Gordon felt it too, that the very system which seeks to deny the shit it produces, also functions because of its shit, because shit always comes back, as Laporte wrote, and must be dealt with, something modern societies have long known at an operational level. The first step in this process, in the operationalization of shit, is the *domestication of waste*, Laporte writes.[12] The domestication of waste was the first milestone in Laporte's account of how shit was absorbed into the machinery of state, I read. Shit became a necessary part of the machinery of state because it could not be entirely removed. Its domestication was necessary because something had to be done with all the shit. To make use of that shit, rather than simply put up with it, was a major advance in social engineering. It made waste production a private concern, something for the privy. As a social excrescence, serving an excremen-

---

12   Laporte. *History of Shit*. p. 28.

tal function, Gordon was clearly vulnerable. Gordon could be scraped up like so much shit and made into a private matter of concern. That was the danger faced by someone like Gordon. The university, or one of its companion institutions, might just scrape him up and look after him. The sweeping up of shit before one's abode, and the potential sweeping up and sweeping in of Gordon once Gordon had been scraped off the street, was not simply observed as a duty imposed by the sovereign. The university and its companion institutions, and underlings, are not merely duty-bound to scrape Gordon up and put him into care. They would become personally invested in the scraping up of Gordon, I felt. The obligation to scrape up shit like Gordon operates at a personal, affective level. The scraping up of Gordon that I envisaged was more than a bureaucratic commitment, a matter of social hygiene, I thought. It would operate in the form of a personal commitment. The scraping up of Gordon would be performed as a personal commitment on behalf of Gordon, for Gordon's benefit, and as such would serve as yet another distraction from the shit piled elsewhere. All this scraping up and distraction by scraping up begins with the Edict, which effectively declares, *mind your own business, and I will mind mine*, Laporte writes. After that it becomes so much more. The tending of doorsteps was an ideological masterstroke. It linked *propriety to property*,[13] but had an outward face too. The tidying away of shit is also performed outwardly, I thought. It occurs in public acts, pious acts, devotional ones. As a social duty, the

---

13   Laporte. *History of Shit*. p. 30.

tidying away of shit begins at home but spreads beyond it. To repeat: The Edict of 1539 effectively declares; *to each his shit*, as Laporte writes. It privatises shit and proclaims *a new ethic of the ego* that entitles each subject *to sit his ass on his own heap of gold*, his own filthy lucre.[14] It sets in place the makings of a possessive individualism, which says, look, *this little pile of shit, heaped before my door, is mine*.[15] That shit-gathering commitment made us what we are, Laporte writes, where *to touch, even lightly on the relationship of a subject to his shit, is to modify not only that subject's relationship to the totality of his body, but his very relationship to the world*.[16] As this last line suggests, the heaping of shit is still done in society. Here I extended Laporte's argument, as they say, feeling as I did so that this extension was an event, minor but an event nonetheless of some significance in intellectual history. Effectively: As I tend to my shit, I look to yours. I'll poke my nose into to your shit too if you give me the chance. The possessive greed of private shit-heaping is connected to a broader social condition, I thought, where shit-heaping is self-affirming in either case. Gordon was at risk of being scraped up as a result of someone's commitment to the commonweal, I decided. The scraping up of Gordon would be their contribution to society beyond the privy, a display of commitment to others that is, in turn, a further act of individuation. It affirms the individual who does the scraping. Ideally, the individual shit-object, a per-

---

14   Laporte. *History of Shit*. p. 46.

15   Laporte. *History of Shit*. p. 30.

16   Laporte. *History of Shit*. p. 29.

son like Gordon, already does the scraping of himself by himself before it becomes necessary for someone else to do the scraping on his behalf. The conscientious shit already scrapes itself up the moment it is deposited. If the shit fails to scrape itself up, it soon falls prey to the good intentions, the personally affirming ethic, of a caring other. The following statement, quoted by Laporte, has to be the most literal interpretation of this shit-scraping commitment, I thought, expressed as a commitment to others wherein all features of shit-scraping coalesce. The nineteenth century socialist, Pierre Leroux, wrote: *If men were believers, experts, priests, instead of laughing as they do at the expense of socialism, each and every one would religiously collect their own waste and hand it over to the State in lieu of a tax or personal contribution. Agricultural production would immediately double, and destitution would disappear from the face of the earth.* Human waste would be scraped up and collected as fertiliser to the benefit of humankind and destitution would disappear from the face of the earth. Surveying the streets of London in their abject poverty, Leroux declares; *every last one of these poor wretches could live off his own manure*, if only they knew the value of it, if only they were organised in such a way to put their manure back into the earth, and so back into production. For Leroux, the necessity of the State as *omnipotent Educator* is here to be emphasised. Left to their own devices, its subjects would *smear one another with shit rather than make a gift of it*, Leroux writes.[17] It was important to teach the people to turn shitting and shit-scraping into a

---

17   Laporte. *History of Shit*. pp. 127–31.

form of gift-giving, he thought, and make a gift of their shit to humankind. Edicts, sanctions, and rules of good conduct would be necessary. They would ensure the citizenry shits to good effect. By implication, waste materials like Gordon must not be allowed to remain unattended. All the shit we produce, that society produces, must be ploughed back into production. This picking up, handing over, or taking personal care of shit (like Gordon), is both efficient and ennobling. Effectively: Look what shit I've swept up for you all. Look at this pile I've gathered to my house so that you may pass by. Here in the shit of others that I take upon myself to gather, in this very heap, in the fact of its existence is my expression of generosity to you and my commitment to society. If only we each did our part and cleaned up a bit more of the shit which piles constantly before each abode, this propertied society would be delivered from itself. Rich philanthropists would be only the most prominent among its shit-scraping givers, proceeding before an army of like-minded folk who scoop up as much as they are able before returning home to sit on their own piles of sanctimonious excrement. Gordon was at risk of being swept up in this manner, out of kindness and commitment to society. That is, perhaps, why he was almost but not entirely shit-like. Though he was definitely *a* shit, and not a little shitty to all concerned, Gordon had already understood and placed himself in opposition to the gift-giving economy of shit. Gordon would not allow himself to be turned into a gift of shit, I thought. Gordon understood too well the nature of modern power, I decided. Modern power can dispense with totalitarian extremes in most cases, because it can rely on a biddable citizenry that will make a lesson of everything and nothing, including Gordon. They would come for Gordon not because they were ordered to, but because they wanted to. In that way Gordon's carers would reinforce the *inquisitorial gaze* of modern power as omnipotent educator. Its disciplinary effects are enforced quite willingly and very simply by *removing excrement from sight*, Laporte writes. *It is enough to enforce a code of shitting—the master's code, the code of he who knows; namely, he who knows how to hold it in*, where to let it out, and what to do with it once it is done. That code of shitting will suffice in most cases. It keeps us in check, where the *master of waste and the warden of souls are one and the same*, Laporte writes, both teach us to hold it in, and how and where to let it all out.[18] A system of good manners, of appropriate conduct and accepted speech, does most of the necessary policing. We learn to hold it in, when to let it out, how to scrape it up, I repeated. This is why Gordon's manners remained poor, even with me, I thought. That is why he was bit of a shit, did nothing to disguise himself as a shit, and yet was not a total and utter shit. It was a finely balanced thing his being a shit. It made sense to me that Gordon was like this. But the sense of what I had just decided about Gordon began to waver as I wondered if Gordon could be explained in relation to Laporte at all. I had very little to go on. All this stuff about Laporte, and about how reading Laporte gives a better understanding of Gordon, is conjecture of the worst sort. The *History of Shit* I was reading was not Gordon's copy. I

---

18   Laporte. *History of Shit*. p. 63.

was reading a copy without prior annotations. My copy was entirely blank when purchased. I read it as it was printed, as if I had laid my face directly under the machine that produced it. I was forced to make my way through this book of Laporte's almost completely unguided by Gordon's prior reading of it. I could not even safely assume that Gordon had read the book, or read it through. He held it closely, that much I witnessed. It was a recommendation. But all I had was this pristine copy of *History of Shit*, and rumours about Gordon that gave the book some context. To make my reading of it more bearable I gave the book a hard time, inking it up with a pen of my own so that it looked as though Gordon had read it, and read it through several times. Because of this reading of the book, as if by Gordon and then by me, the copy I now had before me was almost falling apart. That felt much better. But even in its depleted form the book was unbearable to me. Gordon resisted study more than ever with this book. It infuriated me to read *History of Shit* without Gordon's annotations. But the fact Gordon resisted study was entirely characteristic of Gordon. It was necessary to accommodate myself to the fact that Gordon was resistant in that way, I told myself. Consider the facts. Gordon simply would not be studied, I decided. I could only ever study traces of Gordon, I concluded. In an attempt to gather these traces, I met someone who had heard of my growing interest in Gordon and suggested we meet to exchange notes, as the phrase goes. How she had heard of my interest in Gordon I did not know, because I kept this interest of mine very private indeed. It was probably my predecessor, I decided. It was his passing gift, I thought, to broadcast my interest in Gordon. All gifts contain malice, and this one more than most. That would be entirely characteristic of him, my predecessor. Even in retirement he was doing me over. Following that last betrayal, I was invited by this former acquaintance of Gordon's to coffee. I met this ex of Gordon's over a coffee I would have done better without. The relentless tapping and vapour making of the coffee machines drives me to distraction. Company worsens the effect. As we waited for our order, she told me how it was that many years ago, back in the nineties, she'd attempted to incorporate Gordon's lesson in a wider study of classroom interaction. She worked then, and is still employed to this day, in the Department of Education. Before we talked about Gordon, we had to get the discussion about recent staff events out of the way. It really was the talk of the university, having now spread to the education department, and from there, to sociology. Two co-workers in the education department, well known to the afflicted members of Gordon's department, were found at their desks. One had been sitting there from Thursday to the following Monday until she was found. The other had been sitting at her desk from Wednesday to Friday. Both were dehydrated. They were discovered as was now usual on their respective swivel chairs. Three sociologists followed; one from Monday to Wednesday, another from Wednesday to Monday and the last from Friday to Tuesday. Nothing could be done to revive them from their stupor. All were put on drips. Reports were coming in from other institutions of similar goings on. Sociology departments in neighbouring cities seemed to have been first affected. This soon spread to the rest of the social sciences, and from there to the humanities, and finally to the hard sciences, as they are sometimes called. In the hard sciences it was hardest to detect, since there was very little difference between this slack-jawed behaviour and the usual behaviour that goes by the name of hard science. I sat listening. Hers was yet another tedious retelling of what we already knew, a ritual exchange that all my colleagues embarked upon. We had to get it out of the way before discussing Gordon. When we finally got to Gordon, which was the real reason for our meeting up, and my only true interest, she told me about the study in which Gordon had been involved. Gordon was invited to participate, and since he had not resisted, or responded, Gordon was incorporated like most other lecturers in the university at that time. This was many years ago. Apparently, Gordon launched his attack as she attempted to sit quietly, most unobtrusively she assured me, at the back of the classroom and observe. Gordon's tirade, as she called it, which was also a tirade against her science, lasted some minutes and became most violent in tone, she said, before it ended as abruptly as it began. The first part existed as a set of transcribed notes she was in possession of, somewhere, but unable to locate and share with me. She could only produce a facsimile of those notes that had been passed around the department, in private, she admitted, and was missing a few pages as a result. The original notes remained unpublished. At the time she simply could not fathom what to do with them, she told me. I simply couldn't fathom what to do with them, she said. So, there was no official account of the event, I told myself, beyond these notes and her recollections. These notes, I decided, were clearly of doubtful authenticity. As she talked, I got the impression that she felt by having been there she had gained privileged access to Gordon. It irked me to think she thought that, and irked me more to think I was at all interested, which of course I was. Perhaps she had seen something of Gordon, I thought, but it was painfully apparent that she had not known what to do with the data she accumulated. She was obviously stupefied at the time by Gordon, and was just as clueless now. She had absolutely no idea what Gordon was but acted as if she did. She sat there having absolutely no idea about Gordon and nothing to say about Gordon that would be of any substance. In such an empty state, a state of ignorance, she sat over coffee and passed me this set of notes by which she pretended to know about Gordon. These notes were not even the original set, I thought, but she passed them to me nonetheless as if they gave some kind of privileged insight. The coffee machines that were by now driving me nearly insane had more to say about Gordon, I told myself, than this pointless exchange. This is a copy of a poor original, I told myself, with pages missing, probably the best of them lost. All I was left with was dross. It had been passed around the department in a most unethical manner, I decided, as if it gave some kind of insight into what Gordon was. It was repellent to think of this facsimile being put about like that and pored over by people who would simply not know where to start when faced with someone like Gordon. Even if these notes were accurate, though I doubted their authenticity, they would not know what to do with them. These notes had clearly caused some amusement. They were shameful too. Gordon came across in a decidedly shameful manner in these notes. I should say, not in defence of Gordon but to complement the picture, that Gordon positioned himself quite clearly, it struck me, in this transcript of doubtful authenticity, not against her, but against what she represented in the broadest sense, as if Gordon were standing not only against her, but against the collective onslaught of academic labour that stood behind her and that she subsequently represented by standing before it. To his audience, very probably, Gordon's conduct was as vile as it was absurd. The way Gordon conducted himself was a clear abuse of power. He was a brute, bilious and unreasonable, his behaviour completely unacceptable to those assembled. But what caused the greatest disgust and confusion was how Gordon, as the notes concluded, returned calmly to his lesson, as if the tirade had never occurred. There was no trace of it in his manner as if it had not taken place. But the notes were poor. They were disjointed in the original, she said, and disjointed in this facsimile. Her notes were not normally this bad, she told me. Normally she managed perfectly decent notes. These were unlike her usual notes, she said, and it was on account of Gordon's brutishness. They were far from ideal, she admitted. They were rather poor actually, she said. These notes were very poor indeed, she said, even in the original. It is very difficult to transcribe when faced with a person like Gordon, she continued. You just cannot write properly in a situation like that, when faced with such brutishness, the effects of which last long after the event. I looked at them. They formed a sequence of verbatim quotes and fragments scribbled down with haste and apparent irritation.

Actually, I detected fear. There was an opening bit in Gordon's tirade about coming here (by which he meant there), coming to observe *The Lesson of Gordon* (I think he put it like that), as if it were available and could be observed. Something about that being her first mistake. She thought she could take a lesson from him that would assist her in her research, he said, she reported. As if it could absolve her science, Gordon continued, to learn from me, he said. As if anything about me could be deciphered by science, she wrote, he said. I am nothing to science, Gordon said. I would be the end of science, he continued, if it could decipher me, he said, which it can't, he concluded. A few further quotations on the nature of science (largely indecipherable) and something in the margin about how ridiculous science must be if it leads to an investigation as destined to fail as this attempt to know Gordon. Science works overtime to gain purchase on reality, and fails, he said. It attempts to describe and improve reality, and fails. Science results in situations like this, in which it fails, he said. Then a whole sequence of words followed that I could make absolutely no sense of in this manuscript of doubtful authenticity. There were obviously gaps in these notes, even where they seemed complete. I could sense that. There was an asterisk after science. That word had been coming up quite a bit, she realised. The asterisk indicated a note at the bottom of the page where by science Gordon meant everything and anything at all that fell under the tread of academic enquiry, she supposed, though the social sciences were clearly at the centre of his attack, she conceded, with the hard sciences being so contemptible, I interpolated, so inhuman in their abjection, that they barely warranted attack and could be left alone indeed, if they did not draw so much income and prestige. To attack the hard sciences struck Gordon, as it struck me, to be like kicking a well-fed corpse. Then further quotations about how it fails (it being science in the broader sense) and about how Gordon knew that. How she was enslaved to science, he said, she wrote. How science would objectify everything but never have the courage to objectify itself in all its futility. The last few words were underlined. Something more about it (science) being without footing, though she and it (science) denied that too, he said, she wrote. Then about how her sort, by which he was referring to social scientists in particular, make such claims to reflexivity but scarcely realise what that would entail, or what that should entail. The word TERROR comes next. Capitalised, and repeated. Something further about how she would see herself in all her failure and the failure of her profession. This realisation, I thought, reading the notes, was part of the terror he advocated an encounter with. Then a bit about how *her waiting for truth* (underlined) *would be revealed as a wait without sense—I would say without end*, Gordon said, she noted—*but you're already accustomed to that. Nothing ends in your accursed quest.* Then there is another underlined phrase. Something about her, and about how she and her profession are *the mechanical arts, engaged in self-worship.* Several more near-complete sentences follow for which I have filled in the missing words, so far as I can guess: *You who made the great monotony of modern research cleave to your souls as nourishment*—was one of them. *You cannot see your church about you as it falls apart*—was another. *All you see is the next problem, which is hardly a problem, not even a step forwards but a tripping up*—pieced together from several fragments. *Even those of you who position yourselves against science are doing this,* Gordon said, she wrote. *You worship yourselves and what you promise to yourselves.* Then something more about how your efforts (her efforts) are self-serving. About how your prayers (her prayers) to yourselves (her kind) and your art (our art) are disavowed but they are prayers still. *This pitiable state of hyperactivity you call research,* he said. And something about fooling about, written near to that. *Where repeated idiocies are contrived as excuses*—comes soon after. *You seek not answers but pretend to, as a pretext for justifying a pursuit that will never end, only swallow up resource*—some of that was interpolated. *All this is a distraction from a truth you still cannot bear*—I interpolated that too. Then something about the realisation that the modern research university will never allow your findings (her findings and those of science) to coalesce. About how they are doomed to a perpetual fragmentation that would be deeply upsetting, nauseating, if it did not bring you (her) and those like you (fellow academics) to a wage, and somehow to a sense of entitlement. *You advance to your own limits but with your backs turned* (A familiar phrase? Foucault?). Then a bit more about how you (she) is unable to see the void into which you (she) retreats as if your (her) industry could somehow fill it up and make it whole. About having no patience for this state of collective idiocy called research and none at all for your (her) presence here as you disrupt my (his) classroom. *Yes it's mine. I will possess this space*— Gordon actually said that, she wrote. *What you interrupt is not the beauty of some moment of interaction and exchange that your presence turns sour. No. Nor is it the opposite. You do not interrupt an educational space, degenerate and in need of help, that your science will redeem. No. You interrupt me*, Gordon said, or she noted down. *You interrupt a lesson in which only I am fully sensitive to the idiocy of your presence. My students have not yet acquired if they ever will a full sense of this futility. They do not yet see the futility of the space in which they study, at least not without considerable effort*—some of that was interpolated again. *It will take years*, Gordon continued, she noted, *to disabuse them of what they have acquired through osmosis. They have absorbed the stupidity of an educational order*, Gordon said, she wrote, *that has us in its grip even as it tears itself apart. We are stuck with it, stuck to it. We are its fools. And that is how your presence* (her presence) *in all its futility goes unfelt by those assembled here* (there). *The optimism of education is of a kind with the optimism of research*, he said, she wrote. *The same futility animates both. It makes fools of us in the worst possible way, the most duplicitous way. It makes fools of us by convincing us of the opposite, using every bad example, every failure as reason for redoubled effort. And that is its malice*, Gordon said, she wrote. But that was years ago, I thought. These words of doubtful authenticity were from a previous version of Gordon. They were spoken years before Gordon retreated into his present mode of being. These notes were entirely useless to me, I thought. There was a commotion behind us and she and I turned to find that one of her colleagues was sitting slack-jawed in the café. He was sat before a to-do list. I left the social scientist in the commotion, saying to myself, these notes were entirely useless to me. I wasted an hour on these notes and would not waste another moment. These first-hand accounts of Gordon were utterly useless, I thought. I was slightly distracted by the staff goings-on, it has to be admitted, though not in a way that would impede my coming to know Gordon. The university was setting up its own psychiatric ward to care for employees on-site, though it hardly interests me. This became the typical response of the university sector. Universities were everywhere setting up psychiatric wards, I discovered. It became an accepted feature of university life, these wards, and the necessity of setting them up. My own institution was particularly proud of its own. Not only was it the first to set up such a ward, it could also boast the most impressive ratio between diminished employees and beds. My university maintained the longest standing and most comprehensive provision of beds for the lowest proportion of incarcerated employees. That index, a ratio of one thing to another, was a source of considerable pride. We had more beds than we needed, and so were always ready, whereas other institutions often had more immobile and desiccated employees than beds. In all other respects it was business as usual for the university sector, whereas my tribulations with Gordon were only just beginning. There were some other traces of Gordon's earlier self that I came across, including some old committee proceedings back when Gordon was still on the conference circuit. He was guilty of a tirade (I have adopted the word despite my better judgement) against one of the keynote speakers, only the last line of which was recorded: You are *the mechanical form of existence worshipping itself*, he had said, or so it was written. It took me some time to track down that line, used so deliberately as a parting shot and familiar too from his earlier tirade in those notes of doubtful authenticity. It comes from Nietzsche's late notebooks. This quote that Gordon used as his parting shot comes from a passage in which Nietzsche holds the nineteenth-century philologist to be exemplary amongst educators as a practitioner of the mechanical virtues. The philologist provides *the pattern of an activity that is monotonous sometimes on a grand scale*, Nietzsche writes. For it has long *been the task of all higher schooling* to devalue the agreeable feelings, suppress sensations of the body, and elevate intellectual pursuits in their great monotony. In his tirade, the one that resulted in disciplinary proceedings, Gordon extended this argument to the professor who was giving the seminar. It was possible for me to develop that argument knowing the context of the disciplinary proceedings, and knowing the context of Nietzsche's remark. I merely had to piece the two together and combine them with what I already knew about Gordon, as if I were Gordon, no, as if I could think like Gordon. No, absolutely not. But it was entirely reasonable for me to suppose what Gordon might have said, I thought. Bent over desk or lectern, or prancing back and forth, the modern professor represents machine virtue at its purest, Gordon might have said, I thought. You, he might have continued, addressing the professor, are *the mechanical form of existence as the highest, most venerable form of existence, worshipping itself.* It is worth noting, Gordon added, quoting Nietzsche, lest we give the professor too much credit, that these mechanical virtues may be practised by others too such as the *state functionary, spouse, office hack, newspaper reader and soldier*, particularly those who are the product of the *higher school system*.[19] But the professor is their most swollen expression. You are their most swollen expression, Gordon repeated, I supposed. I had no idea how long Gordon's tirade lasted or how much I would need to interpolate. To err on the side of caution, as they say, I left it at that. My thought was unusually clipped in any case, more so than usual. Conditions at work were becoming unstable, a nuisance, since the instability at work impeded my study of Gordon. With so many employees off sick, permanently housed in the psychiatric ward of each institution, there was no way in which they could be replaced. There was too much for the rest of us to cover, and so universities began to close some departments in order to prolong others. The education department in my university was one of the first to disappear, along with many others elsewhere. It was as if the sector already knew that education was ending, and so the study of education, which was the apparent concern of these departments, was no longer necessary. It was entirely to my benefit that education should be shut down, I thought, since the department was forced to empty out its contents in preparation for its closure. The entire contents of that department gradually appeared in skips. I spent many evenings rooting around in those skips looking for traces of Gordon. Every day after work I would pass these skips by and check to see if there were any new deposits. I would then return later, much lat-

19   Nietzsche, Friedrich. *Writings from the Late Notebooks*. Cambridge: Cambridge University Press, 2003 [1885-1888]. p. 176.

er, when all employees but those housed in the psychiatric ward had gone home. Old recordings were being thrown out, I discovered. Audio-cassettes of lectures given by visiting speakers could be found here and there among the rubbish. I came across snippets at the end of some of these recorded lectures that included time given over for questions. I discovered that in the eighties Gordon was a frequent attendee at lectures given in the education department, though he was not employed in that department and had no real business being there. It was as if Gordon was devoting particular attention to educational matters at that time. Most of what I discovered in these recordings, through which I trawled looking for interventions by Gordon, was pieced together from what the speaker said in response to what Gordon said. What Gordon said, like most other comments or questions from the audience, was inaudible in the recording. I assembled the short attacks that Gordon delivered, for these were never questions, only attacks, from such responses to Gordon as I was able to find, and from what I already knew of Gordon's mode of thinking. *There is nothing to celebrate here but the speaker's vanity*, was one such attack. And: *Can't you see how the celebrated academic has become a ridiculous stand-in for the promise of enlightenment, a promise we still await.* Or another: *All this complaining about the imminent demise of the university at the hands of business is mere lobbying for funds.* And a longer one: *We talk about big names, the most famous representatives of each field, because science has failed us.* And another: *We can't serve science without promoting ourselves.* And: *Our belief in science is not sufficient to nourish us in anonymity.* Or a shorter version of the same argument, delivered a year later: *Our obsession with leading academics is a citation of lack.* Two weeks later: *The international renown of today's academic has become its own justification.* A few weeks after that: *We have distracted ourselves from the real issue at stake here.* And his last recorded remark: *This is it.* Or so I gathered by interpolation, given the nature of confusion his last statement caused. I had a sense that Gordon was not a stranger to this rhetorical form. He was given to delivering pointed attacks or spitting bile. I could not confirm my suspicion since most who worked with Gordon in the eighties and nineties were now retired or working abroad, driven out perhaps, by Gordon, or if they remained employed had become insufferable bores. Nothing was left but these remnants. I piled up the cassettes neatly in my office and looked at them. They are the last evidence of Gordon's bilious phase, I thought. Gordon had left behind his bilious phase and along with it any attempt to convince others of their futility, I decided. Gordon once indicated a reason, or what might be taken as a reason for why he abandoned the tirade as a mode of expression. He indicated to me why he eventually left his bilious phase behind, if that is what happened, by carrying a book, the book I next saw him with and through which I encountered the next phase of study, the crucial phase in my study with Gordon. I saw him carrying that book as we walked alongside one another. Gordon is walking with a copy of *Gargoyles*, I thought. I must read that book as soon as Gordon returns it to the library. As I looked at that book under his arm, I pleaded with no one in particular, and begged, wanting this copy of *Gargoyles* to be absolutely saturated in Gordon's green ink.

Gargoyles is one of Thomas Bernhard's earliest novels, an author who was to become my obsession. Before Gordon I hardly knew his writing, or if I thought I knew it to some degree, hardly did. I checked *Gargoyles* out of the library as soon as Gordon checked it in. There was some ink in the book, not as much as I hoped, though enough to begin with. The book opens with the death of a schoolteacher *found dying and left dead*, Bernhard writes.[20] In the last months of this life this schoolteacher *developed an astonishing gift for pen drawing*, writes Bernhard. He *drew a world intent on self-destruction* that terrified his parents who were looking after their son, already ruined at the age of twenty-six. He drew *human tongues ripped out by the roots, eight-fingered hands, smashed heads, extremities torn from bodies* and so on. As the bony structure of his skull became more and more prominent, the schoolteacher developed a surrealism that was *completely original, for there was nothing surreal in his drawings; what they showed was reality itself.*[21] That teacher needs no more assistance from me, Gordon wrote in the margin. He is already ruined by what he sees. Unlike Bernhard, or Bernhard's teacher, Gordon would draw portraits of teachers who are not yet quite ruined, I thought. He would draw teachers who do not yet know that they are ruined or about to be ruined. These teachers, drawn by Gordon, do not know just how far they are gone, although they suspect the world that formed them and made them teach on its

---

20   Bernhard, Thomas. *Gargoyles*. Chicago: University of Chicago Press, 1986 [1967]. p. 3.

21   Bernhard. *Gargoyles*. pp. 55-6.

behalf is grotesque. They are haunted by that suspicion, by the idea that their mission is equally monstrous and beyond redemption. These teachers are the teachers Gordon would draw, I thought. I suspect Gordon once hoped to achieve such a portrait of the teaching profession. It would have been a portrait of the teaching profession to end all portraits, as they say. It would have ended the profession by depicting it in its complete monstrosity. That portrait would have been Gordon's last intervention, taking years to compose, demanding the most relentless commitment. After its completion there would have been nothing more to do. Gordon's portrait of the teaching profession would destroy everyone he knew and worked with. Against it, the tirade was a mere warm up. But Gordon switched tactics, I thought. He abandoned the thought of drawing, as he abandoned the tirade, once it became clear to Gordon that the teaching profession was already destroying itself quite effectively without him, though it was doing so in the most deplorable way. It was destroying itself without ever confronting the destruction it wrought against itself. It continued to exist or half-exist within a belief system that was atrophied but still functional. Gordon realised, I suspect, that the destruction of the teaching profession was inevitable. Our task was to embrace its destruction. Abject despair was not Gordon's aim. Gordon did not want the teaching profession to confront the destruction it enacted and then give in to unmitigated gloom, which is why he abandoned the thought of a perfect portrait of the teaching profession, I thought, and so failed to confront the profession with the true extent of its deplorable condition. That Gordon had something else in mind became clear to me when reading another of Bernhard's books, also carried by Gordon. He returned the book to the library, and I checked it out. Again, there was some green ink, enough for me to focus on what was important about this book and disregard all else. In this book, the narrator's conversational partner realises the absurdity of human existence and becomes consumed by it to the point of self-destruction. *Everything that is*, she says, *is a lot more terrible and horrible than described by you.*[22] Once again, the significance of this passage for Gordon was transparent to my mind. It related to Gordon's portraiture. As he drew portraits of his own, Gordon risked prompting this condition in others. Gordon risked complete and utter dejection. He could not deliver his final portrait of education to others without inspiring total despair. His tirades were vicious and to the point, but Gordon was only warming up. He was readying himself to deliver a portrait of the teaching profession that would finish it off. As Gordon worked himself up, and perfected his portraiture, he was largely ignored, or when noticed was vaguely indulged, which is another form of dismissal. Many of the recorded responses to his tirades indicated such dismissive tolerance. Gordon found himself in a position where his only recourse was better, more brutal portraiture. The only thing Gordon could do was to develop a more perfect portrait depicting the destruction of teaching. Gordon found himself trapped, I thought, drawing ever more vicious portraits of the teaching profession, perfect-

---

22   Bernhard, Thomas. *Yes*. Chicago: University of Chicago Press, 1992 [1978]. p. 132.

ing his portrait of the teaching profession, so as to prompt in that profession a realisation of its abject destiny. Gordon would not resort to consolation, or hope, or other deceptions. He remained blunt and determined. I pressed on with the book by Bernhard, which seemed now to be a book about nothing but Gordon's tirades and their limits. The narrator survives, I thought, because he seeks nothing more than a break in his condition, only the *attenuation of my state of sickness*.[23] This sickness is deeply rooted in *everything that was around me, in my whole environment*. The *remotest environment* could be *blamed for the fact that I had been precipitated into such a state of sickness*. This world *in all its manifestations* is bent upon *destroying and annihilating me*.[24] *My existence*, Gordon underlined, *is pathological, a sick one. My work*, he underlined once more, *is useless and a failure*.[25] This man, as Gordon understood, clings to life in the most ridiculous and shameless manner. But he does not cling to life in hope of redemption. Temporary respite merely allows him to observe the objects in the room about him *without being crushed and stifled by them*, I read. When his sickness was more pronounced the objects in every room had that effect. The objects in every room would crush and stifle him. He saw in those objects *the worst horror and atrociousness* of existence, finding the *whole shamelessness and appallingness of the world* in the objects that surrounded him.[26]

---

23   Bernhard. *Yes*. p. 59.
24   Bernhard. *Yes*. p. 61.
25   Bernhard. *Yes*. p. 65.
26   Bernhard. *Yes*. p. 74.

They bore down upon him and crushed him. His *receptivity* to the absurdity of the world was fine-tuned,[27] but this very receptivity also saved him, or so it struck me, where nothing but total receptivity was required for survival. A fraction of that receptivity would have been fatal, where half receptivity, or quarter receptivity, would never suffice. His receptivity was total, which meant he knew, he understood, that he could not possess all the futility he perceived and take it upon himself as if it were a matter for his conscience. That is why he benefited so much from the company of those who did not recognise his condition, I thought. They did not relate to him as if his sickness were his condition alone, to own. *As a result of my being ignored*, by them, *together with my problem*, they *saved me*, Gordon underlined. There was an *immediate calming of my emotional and mental state*, Bernhard writes, as a result of his being ignored.[28] There is a lesson there, I thought. Here is Gordon's lesson, I decided. Here is how I will survive my portrait. And with the innate idiocy of a practising academic I had no sooner had this thought than I was having the thought of publishing it as an academic paper on Bernhard and the appallingness of the world. But this hope, which was nothing but an intellectual reflex that all academics acquire, gave way to my equally habitual lament. This thought could never be published as a research paper, I thought, since the idea of the appallingness of the world, and the necessity of total receptivity, rather than half or quarter receptivity, would not stand close

---

27   Bernhard. *Yes*. p. 64.
28   Bernhard. *Yes*. p. 113.

inspection. It would not stand inspection of the academic kind, and if it did, it would only do so as the quoted words of another, as words to be picked over rather than confronted. I was prone to such lamentation, something Gordon anticipated. The next time I saw him, *The Antichrist* was tucked, quite snugly, under Gordon's arm. When I finally retrieved the book from the library, I discovered there were few annotations in this copy of Roth's *The Antichrist*. I could clearly see from what Gordon did underline and annotate that Gordon would tell me there was nothing unusual about my lament regarding writing. Writers before you have endured the *Master of a Thousand Tongues*, he underlined. Like you they suffered a master who tells you to write and sends you out in the world with that instruction, but on your return refuses what you have written as you would wish to write it. They sought to report what they saw, heard and understood of the world, but he engaged them, as he engages you, in a war of attrition. They saw how he took *one of the numerous red, blue and green pencils that lay on his desk*, Gordon underlined, *not so that he might write with them but only that he could strike with them, and he thus struck out all the truths from my reports so that the world didn't learn it was terminally ill*. Obeying this master of tongues, our doctors became our educators, our educators became our researchers and our researchers became our doctors. They will not tell us that we are dying. They will not even allow us to tell ourselves that we are dying, in print. Instead they offer remedies, where educational remedies are the most deceiving. At its best, which is when education is at its worst, educators know their patient so well that they understand exactly, Gordon underlined, *in which of its limbs and body parts the world is weakest.* These weakest parts, being our most tender parts, are manipulated with greatest care. It is *towards the weakest limbs* that our best educators are most gentle, I heard Gordon say as he underlined that text. Education in its most humane, least instrumental manifestations applies itself and offers its remedies in this way. Education applies its medicine to our weakest parts with tender love. We do not learn that we are sick or how far we are gone. That is what sickens me as it should sicken you, Gordon said, I thought. He said that, I thought, by way of conclusion to this most peculiar book, written as a warning in the thirties, *that one might recognise the Antichrist in all the forms in which he appears.*[29] I was surprised to find that others were reading education in this way, as if education were tantamount to the Antichrist. But Gordon's reading of *The Antichrist* was a distortion of a book that believed in education still. Gordon read this book in the most selective way. Only by reading selectively could Gordon engage with education as he saw it because nowhere was education written about as he understood it. Education is not listed in this book on *The Antichrist* as one of its many forms. Gordon had entirely distorted the book by assuming education was identified in it as one of many manifestations of the Antichrist that it went on to identify. For that reason, and following Gordon's distortion, the book was of limited use. Beyond Gordon's distortion of *The Antichrist*, the book was entirely useless to me.

---

29   Roth, Joseph. *The Antichrist*. London: Peter Owen, 2010 [1934]. pp. 72-3.

Because of its limited use to Gordon, his annotations were sparse. There was nothing to do with a book like this except subject it to a brief, but conclusive distortion. I returned to *Gargoyles*, the insomniac Prince, and his Doctor, and persisted with the book until I was utterly exhausted. Unlike the rest of humanity, Bernhard writes, which has *a numbing incapacity for perception, incapacity for observation, incapacity for receptivity*,[30] the Prince heard fatal noises, and spent so much time in *their catastrophic company* that he was considered mad. He would hear these fatal noises almost continually now, and not only hear them, he saw and felt them too, *feeling his brain painfully as a membrane abused in behalf of all mankind*.[31] Against the sound of *crumbling, cracks, tears*,[32] *the tendency*, our tendency, Gordon underlined, *is directed entirely toward death*. If only our teachers were not dead to that realisation, Gordon indicated, they would tell us. But *our teachers have left us*, the Prince said, Gordon underlined.[33] Though the Prince was so deranged he could hardly think, he managed to convene a short conference in which those assembled followed the explanation he gave *of a monstrosity within the universal physical and chemical machine, a monstrosity that was steadily taking possession of all of us*. The conditions at that moment, in which he delivered that explanation, had been unusually favourable for the Prince to share the fruits of his receptivity, Gordon not-

---

30   Bernhard. *Gargoyles*. p. 123.

31   Bernhard. *Gargoyles*. pp. 108–9.

32   Bernhard. *Gargoyles*. pp. 122–3.

33   Bernhard. *Gargoyles*. pp. 178–9.

ed. But the Prince knew that he had become a non-entity, that he *was no longer there*, for his people. His torment was absolutely unknown, completely unrelatable, and certainly untreatable. *My torment is a torment beyond your grasp*, he told the Doctor.[34] I felt myself on the horns of a problem, as they say, but equally felt completely done in by the books Gordon was having me read. I longed for green ink, but at the same moment dreaded it. It was about this time I came across a room full of books in my department. Due to recent events, all departments were being moved into open-plan offices, a cheaper and quicker system for identifying catatonic members of staff at the moment of paralysis. The sheer expense of rehydrating staff discovered days after onset launched the university into this easy and efficient architectural solution. Drips would become a thing of the past at a huge cost saving for the university. Our university would be the first to operate entirely without drips. *Our university: the first without drips* went the strapline of the accompanying press release. That was not the only advantage. The open-plan solution served another important function. It emptied the university of books. With little space to stack them, books were largely eliminated. There was no capacity to move our books to the new offices we were told. Instead, we could take them home, or deposit them in an empty office on the first floor, after which they would be pulped, most likely, some of which pulp would become compressed cardboard covers to entomb any new academic books we published. I walked into that room with my own pile of use-

34   Bernhard. *Gargoyles*. p. 118.

less books to donate, and found myself sitting there with all these books. They were arranged in little piles and covered almost the entire floor. It was a relief to be surrounded by so many books, I thought, and know that none of these books contained annotations by Gordon. There was nothing for me to do in that room full of books. I just sat there amid these books, books that were nothing but the discarded intentions of their owners, books whose owners had finally decided they were nothing but pulp. These books were entirely devoid of interest. I could rest up knowing there was nothing in these books that would tell me about Gordon. It would not last, the bliss. I soon glimpsed Gordon with another book in his armpit. After a short while I checked it out of the library. In this book Gordon indicated a second reason why he abandoned the tirade. Perhaps there would be a third, fourth, fifth, and so on, each failing to explain the condition of someone who has given up on critique, who no longer believes we can critique our way out of our current predicament. Critique, for Gordon, had become a senseless activity unable to face up to its own futility. Critics, as Gordon might have said, devastate themselves unknowingly. It was beginning to rain. Gordon seemed oblivious as he walked with *Wittgenstein's Nephew*. As Gordon made his way along the path in the hollow *Wittgenstein's Nephew* gathered moisture, stuck there in the pit of his arm. The copy I retrieved from the library was in a poor condition. The book depicts two critics. Each critic, the narrator and Wittgenstein's nephew, pits himself against everything in the world, working himself up to such *an extreme pitch of rebellion against himself and the world around him* that his existence in society becomes impossible, Gordon underlined.[35] Each may only return to the world, Bernhard writes, after being taken in by a clinic, one specialising in lung disease the other in madness. To be effective, treatment must systematically ruin each patient. Each patient must become completely weakened by his treatment. He must be wholly done in by the treatment offered him by the clinic, and only then released back into the world. Each man is first ruined and then returned. They return to the world in a weakened and hence liveable condition. The difference between them, however, is that the critic who suffers lung disease exploits his condition when he is released, but submits himself to the clinic when in recovery. When convalescing he relents and becomes docile. He plays the part of the *considerate, unobtrusive, self-effacing patient, the only part that can make sickness endurable for any length of time.* Bernhard knew, Gordon said, that when in recovery *misbehaviour, rebelliousness, and recalcitrance seriously weaken the system, and no chronic invalid can afford to sustain such conduct for long.*[36] Gordon's sickness, I was tempted to extrapolate, was similarly chronic. It was a sickness at, and also a sickness of society, at and of education in particular. Gordon had long acquired the knack of being long-term sick. Gordon was so good at being sick he no longer needed to convalesce. Gordon's rebellious nature no longer worked itself up to such frenzy it near destroyed him. He placed himself

---

35   Bernhard, Thomas. *Wittgenstein's Nephew*. Chicago: Chicago University Press, 1990 [1982]. p. 20.
36   Bernhard. *Wittgenstein's Nephew*. p. 15.

beyond the grasp of the clinic in that way. Gordon's rebellion did not reduce itself either, so that it became a form of low-level disorder. It did not reduce itself at all. Nor did it become a simple source of inertia within the system. Gordon was not a reluctant or grudging participant in the machinery of power. He was not the sort of critic that can only slow down but never interrupt what it abhors. Gordon was sick, but he was also a sickness. Gordon was the manifestation of a sickness from which a sickness of his own, the sickness of Gordon, would spread. The more I knew Gordon, the more I became sick with Gordon. The sicker I became, the better I understood Gordon. His sickness became my sickness. Through his sickness I better appreciated the extent to which Gordon's sickness was my own. My sickening was the inevitable outcome of Gordon's undoubtedly more advanced condition. I realised that his sickness, which I claimed to possess, was not mine to possess, nor was it his. We were just spreading it about. It was inevitable that we should become sick. I could perceive that clearly. Only our rate of decline differed. We suffered it differently, I thought. Gordon undoubtedly suffered his sickness far better than I suffered mine, where Gordon's conception of disease, via Bernhard, reminded me of Laporte's approach to shit, in which our relationship to shit is revealed in its ambivalence. It was a wrench returning to Laporte, but *Laporte on Shit* had something to say about *Gordon on Sickness*. We must attend to this relationship, Laporte seems to argue, where shit is not always an object of loathing, but is given its uses. Shit can even be made profitable. In the sixteenth and seventeenth centuries, Laporte writes, there was still *wickedness in shit*, so it was believed. Nonetheless, once its noxious traces are given time to dissipate, human waste serves as a second-rate fertiliser after pigeon droppings. In the nineteenth century, human shit ranked second to none. In medicine, *attentive scrutiny of excrement*, its *shape, colour, and other features* offered a *tangible index of the patient's body*, Laporte writes, where a good stool indicated wholesomeness. Due attention to this ambiguous relationship, I thought, can give way to a more productive engagement with the shit we produce. A better understanding of our entanglement is one that recognises how we are always *hopelessly soiled*, just as we are always hopelessly sick, and there is nothing unusual about that.[37] Shit is inevitable. It happens to us and we make it happen. What we can do something about is how we deal with the inevitability, I thought. Gordon knew that he was inevitably diseased, I decided. To the extent he had a choice, to the extent he gave himself a choice, it was of choosing the course of his illness, the rate of decline, the mode of decline. Which sounds bleak, and it is, but only to those in denial. Actually, Gordon was more cheerful than most, I thought. Although Gordon had given up on most things including his status as a critic, he had not yet given up on laughter, I felt. I suspected Gordon laughed frequently, though silently. He knew, as Laporte writes, how *all that tumbles* following critique *are a few masks*. The sound of them falling is less important than *the derisive laughter that pulls them down*, Gordon under-

---

37   Laporte. *History of Shit*. pp. 34-6.

lined, after all *they are quickly retrieved.*[38] Gordon was diseased, yes. And there was nothing unusual about that. But Gordon was not depressed. I could see in Gordon (and wanted to imagine in myself) the workings of a dark humour, so bleak most would strain to detect its levity. I'd never seen Gordon laugh. But I felt his laughter. The closest he'd come to laughter in my presence was a fit of coughing. Or sneezing. No. It was coughing. Definitely coughing. I sneezed. Gordon coughed. I think by sneezing I was attempting to distinguish myself from Gordon. The effects of his thinking and Gordon's presence in my mind were exerting a strain upon me. It strained me to be with Gordon. Though we shared a point of view, Gordon was further advanced in actualising it than me. I had not yet, and perhaps never would entirely overcome my attachment to education. Gordon was tearing himself away. He was tearing away from me. There was no keeping up with Gordon. It frayed my nerves to be with him. I would approach that path reluctantly though I was drawn to it too, hoping to see Gordon whilst dreading the encounter. The next time I saw Gordon, suffering my usual mix of trepidation and anticipation, he was following the path below mine as usual. He would walk along that path and I would walk along mine until my path finally descended into his. I noticed a book trailing from his bag, which fell. I cut through the trees and scrub, and made my way down the bank to the book. It was a copy of *Extinction*, yet another by Thomas Bernhard. It felt heavy with green ink, or so I told myself. By the time I retrieved the

---

38   Laporte. *History of Shit.* p. 134.

book Gordon was gone. Several days passed, perhaps weeks, before we met again and before my attempt to return the book. Enough time to read it then, and pay attention to the various passages Gordon underlined. My pace of reading had slackened against my growing administrative responsibilities. It was impossible to read in the open-plan office, and by the time I returned home I was exhausted. My department was facing closure. We had doubled our workload in a bid for survival, or at least doubled the intensity with which we talked about our workload, which can amount to the same thing. The only secure department was psychiatry. It had prospects. Jobs on the psychiatric ward were frequently advertised. For job security you trained as a psychiatrist, though we were all trainees in a way. Our basic training amounted to the ability to spot a colleague as soon as they became catatonic. The first to spot a catatonic colleague received a small reward, a little bump in the pension. At work we spent most of our time carefully watching one another for the first signs of catatonia. That is what university work had become. University workers were by now largely employed to watch one another, though by watching each other so closely we all looked pretty catatonic, making it ever harder to spot the signs of real catatonia. When we were not talking about how much we had to do, we would just sit there in our open-plan office watching one another for the first signs. Our university was the first to dispense with drips. We read that in the press release. We heard it repeatedly in university meetings. *We were the first to do without drips*, they said. Our university is famous as the first to operate entirely without drips, we told ourselves. We had to maintain that reputation for the sake of our institution and spot catatonia when it first appeared, besides there was a small bonus for doing so. It was impossible to read and watch at the same time. So I read *Extinction* very slowly indeed, and did most of that reading in the toilet cubicle at work. Most thinking and much else at work must be done in toilet cubicles. Toilet cubicles are about the only place where thinking can happen, I thought, where the association between thinking and shitting seemed entirely appropriate to my deplorable state of mind. It was unbearable to read a book like *Extinction* that slowly. Only so much time can be spent in a toilet cubicle before one leg goes dead, followed by the other. It is easy to spot these toilet cubicle thinkers, I thought. They walk around with one dead leg from too much sitting on the pot. They think for the amount of time it takes for one leg to go dead, I thought, but not the other. Being habitual toilet cubicle thinkers, they leave the cubicle before the second leg goes dead so that they have one leg to hobble with. Becoming an experienced cubicle thinker myself, I only read *Extinction* in one-leg sittings. This book, which I hardly managed to read, but persisted with nonetheless because that was my sickness, is the testimony of Franz-Josef, heir to an Austrian estate called Wolfsegg. That name, Wolfsegg, had been struck through by Gordon at its first occurrence and replaced by *my university* followed by a question mark. The margins on this edition were extremely narrow so that any notes Gordon made were highly compressed and virtually indecipherable. It was impossible to know what he had written in many cases, though I could tell when he was having a thought, prompting me to attempt my own in similar places. On the last page of the book, under a printed note to do with the typeface, Gordon listed the shelfmarks of a number of other books from our library, which I then retrieved. Visiting the library was not a shameful or embarrassing experience for me, though it is rare for an employee of my university to go there. What I was doing was certainly unusual. Even outside the library, to hold a book at work, or walk around work with a book, or even become known as someone who has a book in his bag at work and sometimes in his pocket is to risk appearing both affected and inefficient before one's colleagues. I try to overcome the shame of being seen with a book and separate myself from its effects so far as I can because shame would reduce me more quickly than otherwise to the routines of university employment. Shame must be resisted, I thought, because of what it would reduce me to. The routines of university employment must be resisted because they become the routines of university thought. The routines of university thought were nothing more than the routines of university employment, I thought. It was insufferable. No, I entered the library with a different kind of awkwardness, the embarrassment of a visitor who does not know well enough, or as well as he should, where to go, and which turns to take. It was the awkwardness of someone not entirely familiar with the environment in which he finds himself, though he should be familiar, has been there before, and should already know which turns to take and where to go. With this kind of awkwardness, which was a spatial awkwardness, I eventually tracked down those books Gordon listed by their shelfmarks in the back of *Extinction*. I traced these books to their respective shelves. To my disappointment they did not contain further notations, or blemishes as they would be described in this context. They contained absolutely no annotations or marks that might have further hinted at Gordon's thinking. It was completely depressing to find myself with these books, books that were clearly indicated by Gordon at the back of *Extinction*. To find myself with books listed by Gordon but empty of Gordon's ink depressed me at the sight of them. I did eventually notice other marks. These helped me cope with the lack of green ink. Once I stopped longing for Gordon's sickly green ink, I became alert to other features of these books. I noticed that certain pages were missing, each being torn in a similar manner, from the bottom of the page to the top. I was led to assume this was Gordon's doing. Where several copies of the same book existed, I looked through them all to find Gordon's adapted copy, or the copy I assumed Gordon must have adapted if it was indeed Gordon who had done what I suspected he had done to books corresponding to the shelf marks written down in the back of *Extinction*. These versions I then compared to the complete editions, reading the excised pages first. Eventually I only read those pages, drawing from them what I could, about Gordon. *Extinction* had already given me something to think about. It was the testimony of a particular extinction, prompted in part by a telegram informing Franz-Josef of the sudden death of his parents and brother. Throughout, Franz-Josef attacks his family, his home, his home country, and all the countries of the north as places where, as Bernhard writes, *everything beautiful is trampled under foot* with the *most appalling hypoc-*

risy. Finding high culture and intellect to be everywhere lacking, Franz-Josef settles into a form of cultural and familial critique that would be extremely conservative, and offensive for that reason, if it were not for its accompanying context. This lament at the lamentable state of culture and cultured beings extends throughout Bernhard's work, I thought, where those issuing the attack are hardly cultural exemplars themselves. Bernhard's complainers do not exhibit those virtues they see lacking elsewhere. They do not embody the beauty of art and the refinement of thought. They are, themselves, ugly complainers. In all their ugliness, then, his critics and complainers offer a critique of culture that undermines itself. Bernhard's own attackers were right in calling him *Nestbeschmutzer*—one who dirties his nest. Bernhard dirtied his nest, for sure. But the nest (Austria) that Bernhard dirtied was never clean. Bernhard fouled his nest only to draw attention to the fact that his nest, their nest, was already a sewer. He dirtied Austria, but in dirtying it showed how much dirt was already there to be found. He dirtied Austria by demolishing the moral high ground of his key protagonists. His ugly complainers undermine the ground upon which they stand. These critics and denouncers of Austrian culture and much else besides have no elevated position, Gordon indicated, I thought. That ground has been undermined, quite simply, by their shortcomings as cultural exemplars. Gordon dirtied his nest in a similar way, I decided. I could see that quite clearly. He lamented *the obliterators and killers*, as Gordon underlined, who were everywhere *killing and obliterating the landscape* of education, whilst being a killer of education himself.[39] Gordon underlined these points in *Extinction*, and saw aspects of his university (my university) in Bernhard's depiction of Wolfsegg. Its highest occupant, the father (our professoriate), did not think any more. Only reacted. Enslaved by *bureaucratic imbecilities* that *seemed calculated* to crush him (them), and his (their) existence, his father (our professors) eventually *took refuge in these bureaucratic imbecilities, I thought*, Gordon underlined. He (they) was (were) *too weak to counter anything, I thought*, and preferred instead to follow *this miserable path leading to total atrophy.*[40] The entire labour force of the university estate was trapped in this way, too weak to resist, finding refuge instead in the procedural idiocies of their work. *Five libraries*, Gordon underlined, *and such hostility to the intellect! For days I walk up and down in my rooms, hoping I'll be able to endure it, and of course it becomes less and less endurable. For days I try to find ways of surviving at Wolfsegg without constantly feeling that I'll go mad, but I find none.*[41] As a teacher, Franz-Josef believes he *must never dissemble with Gambetti*, his student, *or take refuge in prevarication.*[42] His commitment to truth, to which he submits himself as a teacher, means he must reveal himself in all his ugliness. He must teach at his own expense. Franz-Josef will not shrink from revealing distasteful and disagreeable things about himself before his pupil. He demonstrates his

---

39   Bernhard, Thomas. *Extinction*. Chicago: University of Chicago Press, 1996 [1986]. p. 57.

40   Bernhard. *Extinction*. pp. 304-5.

41   Bernhard. *Extinction*. pp. 56-7.

42   Bernhard. *Extinction*. p. 68.

incompetence as a thinker. He admits that the more he studies the work of Nietzsche, Schopenhauer, Kant, and so on, *the more helpless I become. It's only in moments of megalomania that I can claim to have understood them*, Bernhard writes.[43] It is the purest deceit to claim we can know them after study, Franz-Josef realises, Gordon underlines (we scarcely know ourselves). The more he studies these thinkers, the less he, Franz-Josef, understands, Gordon underlines. Franz-Josef attempts to say something about these philosophers in his capacity as Gambetti's teacher, but realises that what he says is trite. At times Franz-Joseph comes out with stuff that even he, Franz-Josef, does not understand moments later. He has thoughts that seem quite clear, and then a moment later they are gone entirely. *Nietzsche, I say, then I tap my head and find it's empty, quite empty. Schopenhauer, I say to myself, and tap my head—and again it's empty. I tap my head and say Kant, only to find a complete void. Though I'm your teacher*, he tells Gambetti, *my mind's a complete blank most of the time*.[44] Most would never confess to this, teachers and intellectuals in particular. We act as if we could take hold of everything, digest it, retain it and convey it. And because everything is obviously too much, when cornered we reduce that everything to prevarication, a minor specialism. This specialism we claim to master. Even then we routinely overestimate what we are capable of. Our teachers spend most of their lives largely blank, I thought. That is what Gordon taught me. Propelled by habit and protocol,

43   Bernhard. *Extinction*. p. 77.
44   Bernhard. *Extinction*. p. 80.

hurrying about, they appear to be anything but empty. We should not be deceived, I thought. An honest teacher would be a destroyer of such conceit, Gordon wrote, including the conceit that makes the idea of a teacher possible. An honest teacher would bring about the extinction of the entire teaching profession. An honest teacher would obliterate every illusion, practice, and malpractice that keeps this edifice of teaching in place, I thought. Franz-Josef comes to a similar conclusion, and Gordon seemed to toy with a similar notion, since his notations, Gordon's notations and marks, were beginning to thicken across these parts of the book. Green ink lay heavily on those pages where Franz-Josef imagines a book titled *Extinction*, the sole purpose of which would be to give an account of Wolfsegg that could *extinguish what it describes*. This book would be *nothing other than an act of extinction*. We would *extinguish it*, Gordon underlines, by *recording it*, so as to free ourselves of it. We carry Wolfsegg (the university) around with us and can never be rid of it otherwise. *Yet most of the time we haven't the strength to perform this work of extinction*, Bernhard writes. *But maybe the moment has arrived*, he continues. *I've reached the right age*, Franz-Josef decides, Gordon underlines. We must give a *substantial account*, he continues, Gordon underlines, *not to say a long account, of what we emerged from, what we are made of, and what has determined our being for as long as we've lived.*[45] We barely have the strength, and it will destroy us, but that it seems to me, it seemed to Gordon, is the only educational task we have left. It was the only educational

---

45   Bernhard. *Extinction*. p. 100.

task, I thought, before Gordon gave up on that too. The ink ran thin. Gordon scratched backwards and forwards at random. He almost tore the page apart by scratching. He would rather scratch about the page than fill his piston-pen, I thought. As I worked through the list of shelf marks and began to appreciate or develop my own appreciation of the significance of the pages Gordon had torn out—to keep or to destroy I could never really be sure—I eventually came across other lists. The books indicated by Gordon's list in the back of *Extinction* often contained the shelf marks of other books. These other books then contained other shelf marks, and so on. The notations were easily missed being much closer to the margin. I was led to inflict further injury on the already damaged bindings to read them. These notations soon took me to texts of a different sort. Instead of the torn books I continued to find, the books were ruined and bashed about rather than depleted. After some careful consideration I took this as a sign of dismissal, or perhaps frustration. My confirmation, as I called it, was a fleeting remark Gordon made alongside the corresponding shelf mark to *that Cossery farce*, he wrote, which surely enough led me to a book by Albert Cossery. *The Jokers* had been almost completely ruined by Gordon. In it Cossery describes a new brand of revolutionary for whom killing or plotting to kill tyrants would be a mistake. Cossery's revolutionary refuses hate: Hate elevates the powerful as subjects worthy of critique. He lives without dignity: Dignity ties the revolutionary to himself; it gives the powerful something to work with, a thing to manipulate. He lacks seriousness: Derision must operate without seriousness. Deride to excess, but lightly, so that the object of derision becomes impossibly comedic. In *The Jokers*, the bog-eyed governor is brought to ruin in this manner, by a systematic campaign of adulation, a cult of the leader launched by the revolutionaries in such a way that the governor cannot afford to disown it. Though he cannot denounce those who claim to adore him, his figure is so grotesquely inflated by their exaggerated support that the population at large and the political class in particular can no longer take him seriously. Oddly, however, their success is hardly desired. Placing the *terrible weapon of irony in the service of the revolution*, Cossery writes, the governor's would-be destroyers are strangely invested in his continued existence.[46] The governor is a pleasurably concentrated distillate, the essence of an absurd society. They enjoy smaller pleasures too, such as the endless, minor absurdities of city living. But these pleasures are always at risk. They may be punctured at any moment by confrontation with human suffering from which even these jokers, in their ironic detachment, are not entirely immune. The governor, by contrast, is so bloated and detestably comedic that the rebel can expect unmitigated delight in the spectacle of his tyranny. That is his attraction, I thought, the bog-eyed governor is completely un-pitiable. So long as the governor exists, the rebel can enjoy uninterrupted mirth. Gordon appeared to see nothing in this book. He would not even misread it as he misread *The Antichrist*. He ruined it instead. But distortion, ruination, and abuse, are all modes of interpretation, I

---

46   Cossery, Albert. *The Jokers*. New York: New York Review Books, 2010 [1993]. p. 55.

thought. It was a matter of working out the nature of Gordon's distortion, which is to establish Gordon's relationship to the book. It was by chance that I spoke to our outgoing union rep on the evening of her retirement, who, being affected by that strange nostalgia which grips people at the cusp of their irrelevance and has them enjoy even the shittiest of times in retrospect, mentioned Gordon as part of a greater reverie that strayed across three decades. Gordon only made a fleeting appearance as *that man* who once took on a rally to the point of halting it. The march was on its way to the vice chancellor's office. Gordon, she said, launched into a great speech, a tirade in fact, *in support of our leader*, as she put it, telling us that our leader was a man of the people, by which he meant us people, that he was a man of honour, by which she meant a man of our honour, and an upright man at that, a fundamentally good man, perhaps even a sage, and without doubt a philosopher in the ancient sense, a man true to his philosophy, but most of all that our leader was an underpaid (we thought overpaid), underappreciated (we thought overindulged) benefactor. Our leader was perhaps the greatest thing that has ever happened to our university, Gordon said, she said, and so on it went. This was the beginning of a sequence of similar interventions, she claimed, with Gordon appearing at meetings and rallies and conventions until at last Gordon gained a following of his own. His panegyric was so consistently flatulent in its claims that eventually she and the other union reps could see a logic at work, a subversive logic, she said, though they didn't agree with Gordon's way of doing things and could hardly support it. But Gordon's following took a direction even he did not intend or foresee, she said. It adopted a constitution of its own, a code that would eventually be absorbed into the unwritten constitution of the university. Gordon's movement and the pompous little article of faith it inspired was taken seriously by the senate, as they call themselves, as an indicator of the spirit of the institution. Viewed by anyone with sense, they said, our institution is a place of wisdom and benefaction. Our university before all others is a place devoted to learning and the improvement of our world. Gordon's movement confirmed that, the senate declared. A derivative ethos subsequently formed the basis of our burgeoning public relations department, she reported, where some of Gordon's clan were to become its first employees. Our leader was delighted, so it was claimed, only leaving the university after serving out one term after another until well beyond retirement, becoming ever more insufferable, for which he was further indulged and rewarded. Gordon's intervention was, then, an unmitigated failure. Gordon's attempts were always abject failures. Gordon failed completely. He made an attempt and then failed. For my sake, I was entirely sympathetic on this matter of his failing. It seemed inevitable that if Gordon should try, Gordon would fail. This further explained, in my view, the origins of Gordon's more restrained, ambiguous disposition. It was not achieved without difficulty, since our outgoing union rep also recalled a more brutal Gordon, confirming the other reports, against which, if repetition is proof of something, a doubtful proposition, our union rep proved the existence of that more brutal Gordon by repeating an image of him that I now knew to the point of tired familiarity. Gordon eventually returned, she said, to the orbit of her activities in the union, having finally abandoned the joke that failed. Gordon was asked if he had any idea how to bring about change if marching and any kind of union activity were still off the agenda, as his actions continued to imply, to which Gordon replied, so she told me, that he had absolutely no idea, and that it was ridiculous to ask him or indeed anyone a question as stupid as that, though Gordon could not escape the notion, he confessed, so she said, or at least stated as if he were confessing something and thereby spoke to her of a thought that had risen to the status of certainty in his mind, namely, that after the various leaders had been taken care of and following them all managers, including those who despise managers but nonetheless do their business, a gradual cull, he told her, is what he envisaged, well, after all that anyone in the world who held a strong opinion regarding how one might change it would either be reduced to silence by some obliterating gesture, or they would be reduced to nothing, a memory, as part of the aforementioned cull, where opinionated types—which for Gordon was a category largely or at least worst represented by those who considered themselves to be educated—would be removed from existence, or at least prevented from burdening it with ideas for betterment that were really nothing but boiled down conceit, a residuum of educated being. He had in mind, especially, though not exclusively, those who work from first principles, since all thought that declares its root in first principles is abject stupidity, Gordon declared, of which academic philosophy, including political philosophy, she added, has to be the most reduced form of organized inanity he had yet encountered, a form of intellectual frottage, he said, she recalled with a grin. This reminded me by some strange association of a giraffe I once saw at a zoo that lowered its great head below the brute next door that was pissing at the time, from which piss it took great gulps, only to raise itself when the piss stopped, and suck inwards as if tasting wine with spittle, a great trail of which spit was carried upon a breeze, together with some half ingested piss, across the face of a woman standing just by me who was gazing at the spectacle like many others beside her. She remarked upon it, referring only to her eye, there is giraffe piss in my eye, she said, no mention of the face, displaying great restraint given the circumstances. I express more disgust when shat upon by a small bird than she did with a face full of piss. The great comedy of her situation, the fact that made it so deliciously grotesque, to my mind, was not just that she had giraffe piss in her eye, but giraffe piss that had been savoured by another such creature and communicated to her upon a trail of saliva. Gordon discovered long ago that his world was beyond perversion, I decided. Weeks passed, perhaps days since I last saw Gordon. I waited where our paths met since this time, as sometimes happens, Gordon was a few paces behind. Gordon approached, then turned and walked past me. I was forced to shuffle a few steps before I was safely in step, whereupon Gordon adopted an irregular rhythm, which made me falter, and this preoccupied me to such an extent that I almost failed to notice another book by Thomas Bernhard under his arm. This incessant reading of Bernhard, prompted by Gordon, was clearly becoming an obsession. That obsession was Gordon's doing, evidently, though I was obviously susceptible to Bernhard's books. It made perfect sense, since Bernhard's books are all about education, I told myself. That is why Gordon reads them, I thought. I was beginning to see evidence throughout Bernhard's books of on-going dialogue with education. Explicit references to education are frequent, legion in fact. Comments on schools, teachers, professors, and so on, are to be found everywhere in Bernhard's work. These more obvious comments on matters educational tend to be the least interesting and most redundant things Bernhard has to say about education. When Bernhard speaks directly about education, most of the time he has nothing much to say, or says nothing worth attending to. Bernhard's educational thought, properly speaking, is rarely labelled as such, explicitly, but can be found in how characters relate to one another. These relationships are grotesque. They are disturbing because they are educational, not despite the fact they are educational, I thought. In *The Lime Works*, Konrad spends *241* pages attempting to teach his wife to *hear*, using the only method he knows. Konrad's teaching is entirely method-driven, or apparently so, like almost everything that counts as teaching today. There must be method, we say. Without method we are without the means to teach. We must distinguish between methods that work and methods that don't. Everything must have method. Method must be teachable, and method must be taught. And so it goes on. But method is also the ultimate excuse, because method can be isolated and blamed. Konrad is exemplary in this respect, I felt. He is devoted to method and deranged by it. Konrad's method-devotion destroys his wife to such an extent he must finally end his teaching of her, and finish the experiment with a bullet.[47] But the truth of the educational relationship, for Bernhard, is not in *The Lime Works*, I felt, but in *Correction*. It was the latest book I had seen under Gordon's arm. Unlike *The Lime Works*, which I already knew before Gordon, I had avoided reading *Correction* for years. There is nothing more off-putting to me than the designation, *masterpiece*. The very idea that *Correction* was Bernhard's masterpiece, or was thought to be Bernhard's masterpiece, entirely put me off reading it. The thought of readers sitting around saying to themselves, this is Bernhard's masterpiece, entirely sickened me and made me never want to read the book. Only Gordon could force me to read this book by carrying it under his arm. I retrieved *Correction* from the library once Gordon checked it in. It was absolutely full of his sickly ink, encircling Roithamer most of all, who is the teacher in this book. The narrator is Roithamer's pupil. He can only be free of a teacher like Roithamer once Roithamer is dead, although even then the pupil is never completely free, because, as the narrator confesses, and Gordon underlined, *whatever Roithamer thought I also thought, whatever he practiced, I believed I also had to practice.* He knew that he had never been a match for Roithamer's ideas, so that eventually *all I could think was Roithamer's thoughts, as Roithamer himself had frequently noticed and found inexplicable, and consequently also unbearable.* The narrator understands the danger of thinking like

---

47   Bernhard, Thomas. *The Lime Works*. Chicago: University of Chicago Press, 1986 [1973].

Roithamer, knowing he is at risk of *deadening himself out of existence* by thinking another man's thoughts. He faces extinction by falling prey to Roithamer's *thought-prison*, and only escapes captivity at Roithamer's expense, once Roithamer is dead.[48] Surely, I thought, listening to what Gordon might say, this teacher is the best kind, which is the worst kind, on an inspirational level. Roithamer is the inspirational teacher in its full form, I thought. In its fullest form, I continued to think. Surely, I thought, Roithamer is the inspirational teacher in its conclusive, concluding form. He represents the inherent negativity of inspirational teaching. Roithamer is the negative core of that kind of teaching. Although the inspirational teacher is today viewed as the teacher in its best form, I continued to think, messianic, I thought, where the teacher who inspires others represents teaching at its best and most powerful in an uplifting, benevolent kind of way, in Roithamer we see the dark, almost totalitarian undertow inherent in that model of teaching. Certainly, I thought, attempting to think whilst reading Gordon's annotations, Roithamer is not an obvious demagogue. Roithamer is far removed from the teacher most well meaning educators like to attack. Roithamer is nothing like the teacher-type educational critics imagine and position themselves against. That teacher—the opposite of the inspirational teacher—seeks to inflict himself on a class, bearing down upon it in the most obviously tyrannical way, approaching teaching as if it were a matter of trans-

---

48   Bernhard, Thomas. *Correction*. London: Vintage, 1991 [1975]. pp. 21-2.

mission, transmitting to others what they must know, where *Mr Gradgrind*, a character from Dickens' *Hard Times*, is the obvious archetype of this kind of teacher, I thought. Roithamer is not a tyrant in that sense. Roithamer teaches by mistake and inspires without intending to. As such, his teaching is almost incidental to his passion for the subject. Roithamer teaches almost accidentally, as if teaching were, in its highest form, a compulsion conveyed to and experienced by those who are in the presence of a compelling individual, a man who has no interest in the activity of teaching and the destruction it will cause in those who are driven to learn. The inspirational teacher in its final form, the teacher who seems to exceed the method-teacher, and who cannot even perceive the presence of teaching in the absence of teaching, is the worst kind of tyrant, I thought. The inspirational teacher in its final form is a Roithamer in the making I continued to think, though Gordon's thoughts were beginning to drown out my own. Gordon's notations and the extent of underlining in Roithamer-related passages had developed and thickened during these thoughts of mine, and made any analogy between the inspirational teacher in its final form and Roithamer's teaching premature. Before long Gordon left me with the impression of a more complex understanding of Roithamer's genius. The tyranny of the inspirational teacher is simple by comparison, I now decided. Roithamer's tyranny is more deliberate and far more developed. Roithamer resists admiration, first of all. People *prefer admiring* others to respecting them, Bernhard writes, where respect in this context means giving due regard to the alterity of those they encounter. They would rather *destroy with their admiration what is valuable in the other person*, since that is what admiration does, Bernhard suggests.[49] Admiration, I inferred, reduces the other person to the evaluative framework of the admirer. Admiration of the teacher prevents the teacher, in this case Roithamer, from disturbing those he teaches, since they are protected by their adulation from his attacks. Admiration prevents Roithamer's companion from seeing or at least suspecting the malice of Roithamer's teaching. To disturb his pupil Roithamer's teaching must itself appear disturbing. It should disrupt or create a disturbance in the educational relationship that binds one to another, I thought, convincing myself that my growing hatred of Gordon was entirely in order. This introduces a suspicion of teaching, a constant fear that *he (Roithamer) may well have meant to destroy me...* Bernhard writes, Gordon underlined, I thought. *I fully expected to be annihilated*, or at least *permanently disturbed* by the effects of his teaching, he continues. Already weak and susceptible, Bernhard's narrator knows, he suspects, that he will become *irreparably chronically disturbed* as a result of this encounter with the last remaining effects of Roithamer's presence.[50] He suspects this is what Roithamer intended. As a thinker, Roithamer demonstrates the recursive and destructive power of thought, of a kind of thinking that is governed by the pursuit of ideas, a kind of intellect that believes *we consist of nothing but ideas that surface inside us and that we want to realise, that we must realise,*

---

49   Bernhard. *Correction*. p. 42.
50   Bernhard. *Correction*. p. 105.

or else we're dead. This is the conceit of educated people, I thought, who believe that *the lack of ideas is death*, as Bernhard writes. They believe that in being educated, they will become immersed in ideas, although educated people are often drenched in nothing but their own conceit. Roithamer represents the imperium of a kind of thinking that educated people aspire to. This kind of thinking demands we become *relentless toward ourselves* (and one another) in pursuit of thought, as we discipline our selves and our bodies in anticipation.[51] Roithamer demonstrates the destruction inherent in the pursuit of ideas, which our best, most enquiring educators, being intellects themselves, have brought upon us and upon themselves. He is the best thinker, and at the same time, the worst thinker. He knows that *a thorough, logical analysis of a subject, whichever subject, means the resolution of that subject*, Bernhard writes. *But we don't, we never think with the utmost analytical rigor*, he continues, *because if we did, we'd solve, dissolve, everything.*[52] Thinking remains haunted, nonetheless, by the pursuit of clarity. And so Roithamer's thought aspires to a level of purity so exacting it must eventually destroy Roithamer once he finally admits that he is not up to the task. Roithamer corrects himself and his work incessantly and to such an extent that the fallacies of his thought must continually surface. Roithamer is eventually *shocked by everything I've just written*, because he knows that writing must always fail to grasp its object. Those who follow Roithamer's example, I

---

51   Bernhard. *Correction*. pp. 138–9.
52   Bernhard. *Correction*. p. 154.

thought, will find themselves *constantly correcting, and correcting ourselves, most rigorously, because we recognise at every moment that we did it all wrong (wrote it, thought it, made it all wrong)*. Knowing that *everything to this point in time is a falsification, they must correct this falsification*, and then *again correct the correction of this falsification* and correct *the result of the correction of this falsification* and so forth, where the *ultimate correction* is a correction we keep delaying. The ultimate *existential* correction, Bernhard suggests, is the suicide of the thinker who becomes the final error demanding erasure.[53] The ultimate existential correction of the educated person who aspires to think, I decided, would be the suicide of the educated person who becomes aware that he or she is the ultimate mistake. The suicide of educated people is the logical destination of educated being, I thought. Roithamer demonstrates the annihilating course of the pursuit of an idea, I thought, and by doing so, demonstrates the annihilating tendency of educated being. Roithamer pursues his idea to the point of death through the construction of a cone as a habitation for his sister. He constructs this building out of love for his sister. This building will, he intends, seek to perfectly represent her inner and outer nature. To realise this perfect representation of Roithamer's thought of his sister in the monstrous edifice of the cone Roithamer must study his sister, intimately, where the study of others is to the destruction of others. His sister commits suicide once she finally enters the cone that was the product of her studied self. Roithamer anticipates this outcome and

---

53   Bernhard. *Correction*. pp. 222–3.

works towards it. He devotes himself to the death of his sister. Roithamer pursues the origins of his monstrous idea, the idea of the cone, and discovers that his idea of the cone is *not* the product of divine intellection—an invention of the mind that will forever adorn humankind—or the discovery of some sort of divine substance we must emulate if we are to rise above our grubby earth-bound being. His idea of the cone is the product of his baseness, Roithamer discovers, which is also, and at the same time, the baseness of all that has formed him. His idea of the cone is the inevitable outcome of a monstrous environment, the formative setting that has made him what he is. *The greater the idea and the higher our aim by way of that idea*, Bernhard writes, *the greater our historical and our familial torments are required to have been*. All that is great and revered, Roithamer discovers, has the lowest origins. Our fortune as educated people, I thought, which is also our bad fortune, is that we can draw upon such a vast reserve of torment, that we have such *enormous capital* at our disposal with the *accumulated capital of torments* that underpin civilization.[54] We are interesting beings because we are troubled beings, as Roithamer might say, paraphrasing Nietzsche. What Roithamer achieves in his pursuit of the cone is the realisation of this torment. Roithamer gives physical and intellectual form to human history viewed as torment. Roithamer is determined to realise and fulfil that torment in his work, in the construction of an edifice that will kill his sister. By realising that torment in the construction of an edifice Roithamer embraces the

---

54   Bernhard. *Correction*. pp. 184–5.

horror of intellection. He does not rise above human history as torment, but realises and brings to expression that torment in himself. Here Gordon's annotations thickened once more. Roithamer's torment was Gordon's torment, or so I felt, since Gordon annotated this book in such a demented and repetitive way that I was compelled to believe Gordon and Roithamer were kindred or at least similar in kind. It was as if Gordon studied Roithamer so closely that he became related to Roithamer in some respect. Gordon was not Roithamer, and Roithamer was only a figure of Bernhard's imagination. It was perfectly idiotic to think that Roithamer's torment was Gordon's torment, and that, as such, they were somehow related, I thought. And besides, Gordon had no cone of his own under construction, or sister to destroy, so far as I knew. But Gordon had constructed an edifice, I could feel that too, using the materials he had to hand, educational materials so far as I could see. Gordon's edifice was an educational edifice. It was the realisation of centuries of educational malice in the malice of one man. He meant to annihilate me—I could see that now. Gordon meant to annihilate me as he approached his own oblivion. And he used books, the building materials of educated beings, in order to achieve that effect. Gordon's trail of shelfmarks was constructing an edifice. His pile of books was designed to destroy me, I felt, by giving expression to the malice of all educational building materials, where books are the most intense and deceptive materials to hand. For this reason, my following of Gordon's shelfmarks, and checking out of books read by Gordon, developed from an obsession and became a disease. My love of books became a hatred of books. I was sick with books but could not escape them. I sought them out more and more, and spent so much time in their company that all I experienced was books, the smell of them, the feel of them, and the sickness that too much reading generates in the mind. In the library where I spent more and more of my time, I developed this chronic condition through the reading of books read by Gordon. Working my way through the shelfmarks and walking down the aisles of books, increasingly sickened by my surroundings, I came across *For the Good of the Cause*, by Solzhenitsyn, once a teacher himself. This book was perfectly timed, I thought, to heighten my sickness. Just when I thought it could not get worse, a book like that arrives on Gordon's sick list. It is an utterly sickening book, I thought. Unbearable. I took the book to my open-plan office where reading was near impossible. In that office I could have a break from reading and thinking. I could sit there and look at my colleagues for the first signs of catatonia. If I spotted one, I would get a small bump in my pension. Sitting there, waiting for my colleagues to succumb to their sickness, I began to wonder about their sickness, and whether or not it was related to mine. We were all sick with education, some more than others, I thought. The psychiatric ward had recently been extended. More rooms had to be found to accommodate catatonic staff. The university had a responsibility to care for its staff, it declared. *Our university leads the sector in staff care*. Fortunately, the psychiatric ward was situated in a building abutting the education department, now closed. It was a simple matter to make a hole in the wall and link one building to the building adjacent, so that, linked together, they formed an extended network of wards. Through that hole patients were fed soon making use of all the rooms released by the former education department. By way of that hole, which provided easy access, the education department was now full of employees suffering the education sickness. The education sickness filled the education department with a record tally of employees. It received inpatients from the rest of the university through that hole in the wall. Sitting there, looking at my colleagues, waiting for them to succumb to their sickness as they looked back at me and waited for me to succumb to mine, I wondered again if their sickness was related to my own. I could not shake the feeling that my sickness was somehow superior to theirs. I sat there, looking at them look back at me and thought, my sickness is superior to yours. I am actively pursuing my sickness, I thought, in books, whereas you are succumbing to your sickness at your desks. I had seen them succumb to their sickness, I had made some of my colleagues succumb to it earlier than they would have done, I recalled with pride, thinking of those colleagues who left our department for the psychiatric ward before we moved to this dreadful open-plan office. I had made them sick, as Gordon made me sick, but in a completely different way. This was proof of their inferior sickness, I thought. Back then, when we were still in our department, in *cellular offices* as they were subsequently called by managers keen to be rid of them, we would each visit one another. My colleagues would stand in my doorway, and tell me, the occupant, that they were simply unable to do everything they had been asked to do. They stood there and told me about those many things that they should be doing, had to do, had not yet managed to do, and would begin to do again as soon as they could. As they stood in my doorway, they told me how when they returned to their offices they found it hard to do the things they should be doing because they were still thinking about how much they had to do, and would begin doing, soon enough, if only they could stop thinking about what they needed to do. I went to their offices and did the same. I stood in the doorway of each office telling the occupant about what I had to do, how I had so little time to do it, and that when I returned to my office I would struggle to do what I needed to do because my head was full of things to do, leaving almost no space in my head to do the things I needed to do. This stopped when, in an experimental spirit, and after a particularly long week of visits to my own office, I went to the office next to mine and began in the usual way. I stood in the doorway and told my colleague how many things I had to do, that I should be doing, had to do, and so on. Then, in a moment of pure inspiration, I finished the usual ritual with the sentence, *but have been unable to do because people keep coming to my office telling me the same.* Immediate catatonia. The truth of it, so simple, so inno-cent, could not be endured. My colleague switched from the habitual pained *listening face* to the *catatonic face*. The dif-ference was small, but perceptible. In the spirit of experi-ment, I tried the colleague in the next office along. Same effect. Immediate catatonia. So I tried another in the next office after that. Immediate catatonia. To test my hypothe-sis with due rigor and method I visited the entire floor of offices. All catatonic. I would have extended my experiment to the entire building, and following that the rest of the university, if my hypothesis extended that far. It didn't. I kept my experiment to *floor eleven*, which is where my hypothesis applied. I cleared it of staff entirely, and sent them all to the psychiatric ward. Alone in my office, on an empty corridor, I expressed a sigh of relief. I spent two beautiful weeks in that office, sighing to myself. When we first moved to the open-plan office, two weeks later, I saw my opportunity. In an experimental manner, I told myself, I would see if I could wipe out the entire office floor, which would have been an entire department, since we were all sitting together in one room. But in the open-plan office our habits changed. We no longer visited one another and complained about how much we had to do, and had not yet done, and could not do because of how much we had to do. If we spoke about how much we had to do, and so on, it would be in the stairwell, or in the common room, but never in the office. We sat there instead, observing each other in silence, waiting for the first signs of catatonia. It was unfortunate that I no longer had the power of immediate catatonia over my colleagues. My rigorous experiment had nonetheless proved to me the superior nature of my sickness. They were sitting there, waiting for their sickness to finish them off. In our previous offices I could do it to them. They were not active in their sickness as I was in mine. I was actively reading, it made me sick to read. There was no putting off *For the Good of the Cause*, I thought. I would read this utterly sickening book because that is the hallmark of a superior sickness, I decided. Some pages were creased, as if once soaked right through to the gutters. I had previously read *One Day in the Life of*

Ivan Denisovich and dipped into *The Gulag Archipelago* like any good student of the twentieth century, but *For the Good of the Cause* was new to me. A lesser known book, a tale of sabotage and betrayal with education as its victim, it is an utterly awful book. As I read Gordon's copy, or the copy I assumed was his, I had the sense from Gordon that the Soviets were right to ban it and work to grind its author into the dust. You could feel Gordon's disgust at the book by how it had been mistreated, where the first pages, describing the teacher Lidia, were particularly rotten. The so-called free world came to the rescue, Gordon hinted, not because Solzhenitsyn's work revealed the inherent corruption and brutality of the Soviet system, but because it appealed to their educated conceit. This book echoed the inbuilt conviction that education is the mainstay of any civilized society. It appealed easily to liberal tastes, and together with the rest of Solzhenitsyn's output could not go uncelebrated, with Nobel prizes and so forth. In this utterly sickening ode to education, the students of a cramped, run down school are encouraged by their beloved teacher, Lidia, to take it upon themselves to build the proper accommodation that the Soviet authorities had promised but never delivered. This becomes their supreme educational task, a task of the most charmingly formative kind, as those involved develop through this endeavour of building their new school the technical and social skills necessary for working in common and for a common cause. The building that is the object of their devotions is almost completed, and then, most abruptly, taken from them. It is repurposed at the last moment, their goodwill is co-opted *for the good of the cause*, which, in the Soviet Union, meant ruthless greed and nepotism. Reading against the grain of a book I was already beginning to loathe, I had the sense that from Gordon's perspective Lidia was a tyrant too. She was the tyrant of the promise of truth, as Gordon might put it. She not only claims to speak it, she exudes it. Lidia is the shining light of education, a beacon of hope, the motivational educator who guides her class to better things. She orients her students to a hope they will never realise though they must exhaust themselves in pursuit of it, digging foundations, erecting walls, and so on. Rendered stupid with enthusiasm for her educational project, these students sing an anthem, an ode to technology and progress, recalling the revolutionary spirit of those who did voluntary work in Lenin's time. Lidia is their lodestone, and gathers students to her side by moral attraction. She is a moral exemplar of such force that none can resist her. *The minute Lidia came out of the room*, entering the crowded corridor of the old school that was about to be replaced, *she was overwhelmed by those trusting eyes and smiles*, Solzhenitsyn writes. *It was the supreme reward of the teacher: students crowding around you eagerly like this. They could not have said what it was they saw in her. It was just that, being young, they responded to everything genuine*, he continues. *You only had to take one look at her to know that she meant what she said*. She commanded absolute trust. Hers was a reign of truth, not a reign of force. Replacing force with truth she achieved the highest, most fanciful object of post-Enlightenment education. Lidia established an educational space from which violence is finally removed. With Lidia revered in this way, as a moral exemplar and defender of true education, *the boys were only too proud to run errands for her. She always accompanied her instructions with a slight but commanding gesture, sometimes—and this was a sign of great trust—with a light tap on the shoulder*, Solzhenitsyn writes. Blessed in such a way, they would run off and carry out her orders, *like ants*, he writes.[55] *Like a general taking a medal from his pocket and firmly pinning it on a soldier*, she would command their obedience. Her level of control was not perfect, however, because Lidia did not aspire to military discipline.[56] As a motivational educator she feared only apathy in her students. She *didn't care how excited they got or how they baited her* at times, for such was her benevolence. On occasion they *howled with pleasure*, for she *never lied*, and always engaged with them. She believed that *people who argue are open to persuasion. What she feared most of all in young people was indifference.*[57] Facing a minor rebellion, in which some of her students argued against the power of literature, she wished only to *calm the rebels. You just wait!* She said. *I won't let you get away with it*, she continued with good humour. *We're going to have a big auditorium in the new building, so in September we'll have a debate.*[58] Perhaps few will find Lidia as abhorrent as Gordon did, I thought, as he wrenched the book between his hands. It is remarkably difficult to disturb this conceit, Gordon thought, or so I felt, which believes in truth as redeemer, and so places the truth-

---

55   Solzhenitsyn, Alexander. *For the Good of the Cause*. London: Sphere Books, 1971. pp. 44-5.

56   Solzhenitsyn. *For the Good of the Cause*. p. 46.

57   Solzhenitsyn. *For the Good of the Cause*. pp. 51–2.

58   Solzhenitsyn. *For the Good of the Cause*. p. 54.

ful educator in all her sincerity at its pinnacle, not realising how much that educator will have first tamed and enslaved her students. From Gordon's point of view, the kindly educator is a dangerous fiction. Educators are beguiled by that phantom. The idea of the kindly educator, for Gordon, was sheer malice. Educators are malicious beings. So-called kindly educators are no exception. Gordon's own malice, as an educator, was only unique for being deliberate rather than habitual. As an educator Gordon gave way to its malice. He turned repeatedly to the work of Thomas Bernhard, or so it seemed to me, because in that work the malice of education appears with unusual clarity. As I trawled through the work of Bernhard, I became aware of a *little imitation novel*, as its author described it. Published in translation under the title, *Revulsion: Thomas Bernhard in San Salvador*, this book indulged negativity and repetition, the former to excess.[59] That indulgence is not Bernhard's lesson, I thought. Bernhard's revulsion was not unrestrained. His revulsion was stoked, as it was tempered, by the heavy realisation that Bernhard himself was a problem that must be overcome. This world cannot be escaped, Bernhard knew, and the folly of that little imitation novel was to neglect this central detail, I thought. You cannot escape El Salvador if that is your upbringing, as Bernhard knew he could not escape Austria, as Gordon knew he would not escape education, not without contorting himself beyond recognition. Gordon could not escape education without the most horrific contortion of

---

59   Moya, Horacio Castellanos. *Revulsion: Thomas Bernhard in San Salvador*. New York: New Directions Books, 2016 [1997]. p. 88.

Gordon. The deformation of Gordon by Gordon was a necessary prerequisite for the undoing of education. And since Gordon existed as an educator by virtue of the educational relationships that status entailed, those relationships would also have to be destroyed. Since they existed and set themselves up regardless of whether he wished them to exist, he would have to contort those relationships too, I decided. I returned again and again to the library in search of Gordon's books, a library that was busy reducing the size of its collection. Situated adjacent to the education department, the library was perfectly positioned to further extend the number of psychiatric wards maintained by the university. Several floors of the library were converted at minimal cost to the institution. As the emptied shelves were pushed together, they formed beds, bunks of a sort—a highly efficient use of space. Books made way for the influx of patients. Librarians worked overtime to reduce the number of books. Walking about their reduced dominion I could see the remaining librarians conducting themselves with the usual gloom of a university employee. Across the lintel at the front entrance was the following quote from Borges, in chalk: *When it was proclaimed that the Library contained all books, the first impression was one of extravagant happiness.*[60] The second and third impressions were less jubilant. A library that contains all possible books is a terrible thing, Gordon would say, I thought. The fact that the university library was emptying itself of books should be a consoling thought, I

---

60   Borges, Jorge Luis. The Library of Babel. *Labrynths*. London: Penguin, 2000. p. 82.

told myself. I should be consoled by it, I decided, as I walked under that quote and into the library thinking of all the books that were being discarded, books I would never have to read. Many of the books Gordon had me read in subsequent weeks I would not usually bother with, such as William Gerhardie's *Futility*. Gerhardie's *Futility* would not even be on my radar, I thought, had Gordon not led me to it. As I sat there with Gerhardie's *Futility*, reading that book, only one of many now piled up before me, I thought to myself how I must look through the eyes of another. I must look very well read, I thought, sitting in the library with all these books, when I should be sitting in my office looking at my colleagues for the first signs of catatonia. I looked like a person of extremely wide reading, I thought, sitting there with books from every part of the library. But it is a mistake *of the first order*, I thought, to believe it a sign of the highly educated to sit like that, before a pile of books from every part of the library. The highly educated do not read books from all parts of the library, I thought. They would never rove from one book to another as Gordon had me do. It is not a mark of the highly educated at all to read like this. To sit with a pile of books like that is to betray one's utter lack of taste, Gordon would say, I thought. The highly educated have a well-developed taste for books. They refined that taste severely by becoming highly educated. To be doing this kind of reading, the reading of a philistine without selective taste, is almost anti-intellectual, I would say, or so it would seem to those with taste. Only a cultural philistine would rove between books as disconnected and mutually hostile as these books before me, books that Gordon had me assemble. It betrayed my utter lack of taste, and sense, to have assembled here, at my library desk, books of such diverse preference. There was a book here for every appetite, I thought, and by consuming them all I showed myself as someone who would dine anywhere and on anything. Feed me any slop and I will read it, these books testified. The pile testified to my utter lack of refinement. They declared to all who passed by that I had no powers of discernment, no idea why one book should not be placed alongside another. The academic class, the habits of which I knew all too well, would never condone let alone encourage such public wandering across a terrain already divided into its specialisms. When academics overcome their reluctance to move between specialisms, they work hard to disguise their mutual contempt. They engage one another in collaborative endeavours that are marked by a persistent failure to share a point of view that goes beyond anything but a superficial alliance. They do not wander between specialisms by reading one another's books. Or if they read them, they pay little attention. Academics only dine with other academics from other specialisms by pretending to communicate with those who share none of their presumptions. These so-called discipline-hopping academics, with absolutely nothing in common but a shared sense of entitlement, find themselves working with one another because it is a quicker route to funding. These academics do not read across disciplines for anything other than instrumental purposes, hoping to make use of other academics, and draw upon their disciplinary capital. Presiding academics must suppress their contempt for these interlopers. These experts have made it their business to pronounce at length on such and such topic, and could make fools of interlopers in an instant. And so, to avoid intellectual disgrace, those wishing to travel between fields must keep their engagements superficial. The university has long considered itself a source of good manners. And good manners are the best cover for stupidity. Between disciplines, there is shared agreement not to probe too deeply, to avoid saying anything much at all that could be contested by individual specialists. Engagements must remain surface deep and ruthlessly instrumental to avoid intellectual embarrassment. That is how our highest class of educated person perpetuates its own specific strain of stupidity, I thought, ensuring that each encounter is mediated through, or at least does not offend the gaze of those who know. The best of us develop a talent for saying nothing much at all about most things at work, whilst saying quite a bit about nothing. In that way nothing is confronted, though everything is talked about. Gordon's list of books reduced me further. Gordon had me rove across boundaries of taste with crude disregard. He turned me into a philistine, or an interloper, I was too intellectually drained to decide. There was no following Gordon without entirely losing one's professional respectability, I thought. I sat there in the library with my motley pile of books and felt professionally discredited by them. The authors were often unfamiliar, the titles new. These books declared my ignorance. No self-respecting academic would sit in a library with such a perverse selection of books, I thought. After Gerhardie's *Futility*, Gordon took me to an entirely different era, through Heinrich von Kleist's *Selected Writings*. Having already leapt a century back to *Futility*, I now found myself leaping another. I strayed between centuries in a manner that would make historians weep. These *Selected Writings* placed me in another period of dissolution and chaos. Following Gordon's trail of shelf marks, I came across a translation of Kleist's works from which the editor's introduction had been entirely removed, torn from the bottom edge upwards and outwards. These first pages offered an account of Kleist's life that bore resemblance to Gordon's own, as I pictured it, though it was an improvement on Gordon in some respects. Having pointed me in the direction of Kleist it felt as though Gordon wished me to cease following him altogether and find lessons elsewhere, in lives more enigmatic than his own. Soon Kleist's life had a grip on me as Gordon's once had, and for the duration of that engagement I hardly thought of Gordon at all. Gordon retreated and became a spectral figure as I studied Kleist and lost myself in this edition of his *Selected Writings* with its torn out introduction. I attempted to extract more than I should have done from this book, taking so much from those pages, the life they described, and the *Selected Writings* they introduced, that the more I studied Kleist, the more I found myself picturing Gordon, until it was finally impossible to read anything of or about Kleist without thinking I was encountering Gordon. Which is not to say that Gordon was just like Kleist, or Kleist was like Gordon. Actually, I suspected I hardly read Kleist at all since there was nothing in Kleist that resembled Gordon. Seeing Gordon in Kleist I was completely unable to engage with Kleist or anything written about Kleist, without misreading it entirely as if it were a description of Gordon. With the library stock increasingly depleted by the influx of patients, and with Gordon's tendency to read unpopular books, which are the first to go, combined with Gordon's habit of prematurely disfiguring those books he checked out and so promote them to the librarian as copies worth dispensing with, I was frequently coming up from my search empty handed. Probably my worst disappointment was a paperback *Bible*, a book that would be full of interest once Gordon gave it his imprint. Churches would weep. But this edition had already been purged. All remaining copies were, needless to say, completely useless. These bibles, all of them useless since Gordon had not touched them, were taking up space that might have saved other books from oblivion, I thought. Each bible was hateful to me for the shelf space it occupied. Fearful that Bernhard's books would be next, I checked out the entire collection, which already had some criminal omissions—*Correction* and *Extinction* had by now been expunged from that collection, and *Gargoyles* was almost falling apart, so surely would be next. There was no record of the library ever having a copy of *The Lime Works*, or *Concrete*, or *Frost*. Unable to renew the Bernhard collection indefinitely, I checked it back in and then stole away with it to the lavatory, from which I dropped the entire Bernhard collection several feet from a tiny window into a hedge. As I sat in my cubicle waiting for the room to become entirely silent, and then for the corridor to fall silent too so that I might emerge from my hiding place and hoist myself to the window, I felt that I should read or at least look at one of the books. *On The Mountain* was at the very top of the heap. Waiting for the room to become silent made reading impossible. Despite wanting to read from the heap of books, I could not read the books on my lap, nor even glance at them, since that would interrupt my listening for sounds including sounds in the corridor, which required concentration. I merely sat in the cubicle listening whilst thinking that I should really be reading since this was a perfect opportunity. A toilet cubicle is ideal for reading, I thought, as I have often thought before. But I simply cannot read if I am listening for sounds. It is impossible to read under these conditions, although toilet cubicles are otherwise ideal for reading, at least for a short while. The conditions at present were perfect, since there were several other cubicles to choose from, and the toilet was in low demand. These conditions are absolutely ideal for reading, I thought. Yet I was completely unable to read under these conditions, since I was not only listening for sounds, and waiting for the opportunity to hoist my heap to the window, I was also preparing to hoist myself up to the small window. If worrying about something constitutes preparation for doing it, I was preparing by worrying, and since I was consumed by my worrying about whether or not I could hoist myself to the window, and do so unnoticed, I was completely unable to read. The entire Bernhard collection (with a few criminal omissions) was just sitting there, inert, on my lap. Most of it was annotated by Gordon, or adulterated in some way and so full of meaning, and yet the entire Bernhard collection (such as it still existed) was just sitting there on my lap, inert. Meanwhile Gordon was becoming increasingly difficult to shadow when I saw him, which was not very often at all. So when I was not listening for sounds in the corridor, or thinking about how difficult it might be to hoist myself up to the window, I was thinking about the Gordon problem. There would come a point when we ceased to meet entirely, I thought, and no sooner had I thought that, we ceased to meet. I would vary my hour of departure, leaving as early as three in the afternoon or as late as seven in the evening. This confirmed the rumour that Gordon was now leaving work at irregular times and led me to an increasingly irregular rhythm of my own. I would better my chances of catching Gordon on his way through the hollow by adopting an irregular rhythm as well, I decided. Sometimes I would encounter him directly, but most often I saw Gordon through the trees. I could see that he was emptying out his office or doing what looked very much like what a man would do if he was emptying his office of books by carrying them away. Often there was a book under his arm, which he would either take with him beyond the point where our paths eventually forked, or Gordon would fling the book into the undergrowth. The first time this happened I saw Gordon from my path as usual. Knowing there was no catching him up as he ploughed on with a thick hardback buried under his arm, I paused to watch. Almost without breaking step Gordon hurled the book upwards and over his shoulder to the right. Already cracked at the spine in numerous places it flew to pieces. After a pause I made my way down the bank and through the scrub on the other side where I began to collect parts of the book. Its lurid pages were easy to recognise. I knew them immediately. Gordon had just dispensed with *The 120 Days of Sodom*. As the remains of the book were in a state of complete disarray, I could assemble nothing of significance or insight regarding Gordon's reading of the Marquis de Sade. Even missing pages were impossible to pinpoint with certainty, and so I left them for the dog walkers and rats. The next book flung by Gordon into the bushes was a biography of Major Charles George Gordon, born 1833, died 1885, killed at Khartoum after a long siege. His death elevated (Major) Gordon to the status of public hero, as if he were a perfect example of the lone Englishman, a man of honour, who sacrifices himself for the glory of Empire. Gordon became a Christ-like figure to his contemporaries, celebrated for resisting the advance of radical Islam. Following his death, public lament came first, then social upheaval and protest against a government that could let him die, a romantic painting *(General Gordon's Last Stand)*, several hagiographies, eventually a film *(Khartoum)*, followed by counter-hagiographies and correctives to these counter-hagiographies, biographies, studies of these biographies, correctives to those studies of biographies and so on. I could not stand it. I had no intention of constructing the life of Gordon (my Gordon). Gordon's life was a disaster beyond the grasp of any biographer. Only one thing about Gordon interested me: how the disaster of Gordon's life was reflected in Gordon's thought, and how the disaster of Gordon's thought was reflected in his life. The unmitigated disaster of Gordon's life and Gordon's thought did not cohere about a point. As reflected in Gordon's thought, the disaster of Gordon's life could not cohere in the thought of Gordon. As reflected in Gordon's life, the disaster of Gordon's thought could not cohere in the life of Gordon. Gordon's thought and Gordon's life would not cohere and could not be understood in their coherence, I thought. Gordon's thought and Gordon's life existed only as a response to the books that he read. To speak of Gordon's life or Gordon's thought as a disaster is already a distortion. Everything about Gordon was broken across the books that Gordon read in all their mutual incoherence. This book, *Gordon: Martyr and Misfit*, had clearly been worked through meticulously, at least mechanically, since every mention of Gordon was struck through horizontally, and then vertically, as if crucified.[61] There were no other notations, only this relentless and repetitive crucifixion of a name in print. The crosses drawn through the book from the first page to the last made a mockery of Gordon's crucifixion, or the thought of his crucifixion, along with the enduring but equally ridiculous thought of Empire. These annotations made his crucifixion banal by over-crucifying Gordon, and destroyed Gordon far better than any counter-hagiography had ever done, I thought. Gordon was over-crucified and thereby ridiculed in this book that Gordon finally threw out. This throwing habit was repeated along that path. It became a habit of my own to descend the bank, after a pause, and collect what Gordon had thrown aside. I was already sick with books and scarcely needed any more to add to my burden. But the contents of his office, if these books were taken from his office, were too irresistible for someone grown accustomed to trailing the mind of another. Gordon had already made me thoroughly sick with

---

61   Nutting, Anthony. *Gordon: Martyr and Misfit*. Bungay: The Chaucer Press, 1966.

books. These final books were only calculated to further my sickness. Carefully chosen to spread the sickness of Gordon, which had me firmly in its grasp, these books were intended for my final, complete annulment. They were stacked against me. I suffered, nauseous with Gordon's books, and reached a state of anguish never before encountered in all my years of reading. These years of reading, full of discomfort and silent animosity, were nothing by comparison. Gordon kept throwing books, and I kept picking them up. Just bending over to pick up his books made me nauseous. The blood flowed to my head that was already sick with books and empty of books. I knew I could not become Gordon, or bear his sickness, my sickness, as Gordon bore it. Some of these books were in a terrible condition. There were hardly any pages left. They were the worst. I picked up a copy of *The Writing of the Disaster*, of which only page *4* remained between the covers. *Let the disaster speak in you*, it said.[62] The books Gordon threw were hard to find. I raced against oncoming darkness to discover their location, and as I tore about through the undergrowth, I felt demeaned. It could be worse, I thought. I could be catatonic. I was grubbing about, trailing after Gordon, but I was not Gordon's disciple, nor was I his admirer. I was not Gordon's lackey either. Thinking in this way, about my not being a disciple of Gordon, I recalled *Old Masters*, another book by Bernhard, read by Gordon and stolen from the library, dropped from the toilet window. The student in *Old Masters*

---

62   Blanchot, Maurice. *The Writing of the Disaster*. Lincoln: University of Nebraska Press, 1995 [1980]. p. 4.

is a kind of disciple, I thought. I am not. It is not my mission on earth to teach Gordon's lesson. Intellectually, that student is entirely dependent on his teacher. He adores his teacher, I thought. That is the problem. He mimics his teacher because the voice of his teacher sounds so clearly in his head. All he hears is his teacher's voice. I hear nothing. When I am with Gordon, I hear absolutely nothing. That student is a disciple. I am not. For this reason, he *still remains the peasant his ancestors were*, Bernhard writes,[63] and he remains the peasant his ancestors were despite working thirty years in the city, in a great art gallery. He remains a peasant despite the intellectual training he has received, from Reger, where Irrsigler, the student, has *over the years, appropriated verbatim many if not all, of Reger's sentences*. The relationship between the two is so close that *nearly everything that Irrsigler says has been said by Reger*, Bernhard writes. Irrsigler is his *mouthpiece*.[64] Irrsigler remains enslaved, intellectually, to Reger, I read. He is enslaved to Reger despite Reger's subversive teachings regarding the impossibility of mastery, the hatefulness of art, the failure of philosophy, and the overwhelming horror of the world. His student, Irrsigler, should have become someone like Reger after so much training, and not simply his mouthpiece. Better still, Irrsigler should have become a denier of art and culture, a modern barbarian, given what Reger taught him. But Irrsigler *remained a peasant*, a peas-

---

63   Bernhard, Thomas. *Old Masters: A Comedy*. London: Penguin, 2010 [1985]. p. 109.

64   Bernhard. *Old Masters: A Comedy*. p. 6.

ant, I told myself by way of consolation.[65] Irrsigler's education has completely failed to transform him, I decided. Reger's teachings have only appended themselves to Irrsigler. What this educational relationship lacks, I told myself, is sufficient malice. It lacks sufficient malice between educator and student, and in that respect it is entirely artificial and completely unbelievable, I thought. It lacks Roithamer's malice, and the student's fear of that malice. There has to be some kind of fissure between teacher and pupil, I thought. Otherwise the relationship is entirely artificial. That fissure between teacher and pupil is where the inevitable malice of teaching sets in. That is what Gordon taught me. This fissure may occur quite naturally, I thought. In most cases there is something about the teacher, about the teacher's teachings and about the teacher's context that is repellent and thereby oppressive. Most often a teacher is naturally repellent in some way, I thought. The inherent oppression of teaching is almost entirely habitual, I decided. The oppression wrought by teaching is most of the time in most cases completely *un*-thought, I thought, and that is the malice of teaching, I continued to think, although in that form, in that unthinking and entirely natural state, the malice of teaching is not what it could be, I concluded. To make this repulsion *deliberate* is another matter. Carefully wrought oppression can, in some cases, be desirable, I thought. And that was Gordon's art, I supposed. It was repellent that I found myself, as I was, trailing about looking for books flung by Gordon. And in these conditions

---

65   Bernhard. *Old Masters: A Comedy*. p. 109.

too. The conditions in which I found myself were awful. Almost without fail it rained. The books were already half soaked by the time I had them in my grasp. I came to fear these wet, disintegrating books. Even more I feared that I might stop finding them, and that Gordon might stop flinging them. I was fearful that Gordon would cease this throwing of books altogether if he saw me spying upon him. As I waited for Gordon, I did my best to remain concealed, hidden on my path and reluctant to appear, making it even more unlikely that we ever met in person. This hiding from Gordon was as repellent as the ferreting about for his books. On one occasion Gordon threw a book to the left, which was my side. I suspect he saw me upon the edge of my path. There I was, leaning forwards in anticipation. Without looking directly at me to confirm his suspicion, if he did indeed suspect, Gordon quickly retrieved the book and walked away along his path. As the rain wore on, the books I retrieved became more difficult to open without damage if they remained bound, and eventually very hard to decipher. The time it took to get a book seemed decisive in determining the condition of the book I retrieved. This did not prevent me from looking for books even when Gordon was not there. The fact that books like that, previously flung books, would be entirely unreadable did not put me off. Believing they might have been thrown into the scrub, and on days that I missed Gordon as he made his way along that path, I spent as much time as I could looking for books, but only ever found remnants of books, nibbled at the spine and so falling apart, or pages that disintegrated as I lifted them, or whole chapters already turned to mush. They were deteriorating fast. This factor, combined with Gordon's increasingly irregular hours, led me to spend more and more of my time there, walking up and down, hoping to increase the chances of being on my path when Gordon was walking along his own. I left work earlier and wandered along my stretch of path later into the evening until I could not leave until the darkness was absolute. Eventually I spent whole days walking up and down that path, bringing work that I should have been doing at work to complete, setting to it along that path where I would fulfil my contractual duties to the best of my abilities. I could hardly concentrate for constantly looking up to see if Gordon might be on his way. My looking up came to resemble a nervous tick, or so it might appear to another. It certainly revealed my anxiety. I knew that this constant looking up habit was perfectly rational. It was a reasonable habit, I thought. This looking up habit increased my likelihood of seeing Gordon well in advance, giving me plenty of time so that I could hide, wipe my eyes in preparation, and adopt a position from which I might see where the next book ended up. Picking the right duration between Gordon's departure and my descent became a matter of painful judgement. The longer I left before descending, the less likely I was to find the book, the more likely it would be that the book, if found, might be in an unreadable condition. Descending too soon, however, might put Gordon off and cease the flow of books from an office that was, I presumed, swiftly emptying of contents. Waiting there, I worked less and less, and began to eat less due to my anxious condition. I could hardly bear the time to prepare or buy such things as would sustain me. And when I bought things, I could not bring myself to chew. Any time not spent on that path seemed to me wasted time. I began to worry that Gordon walked and indulged in the throwing of books when it was dark. Why not? I wondered. Despairing it had not occurred to me that Gordon might be throwing out books at all hours I found it hard to sleep at home, and frequently woke in the middle of the night, drawn by this dread of rotting books to night-time wandering up and down the same path where I now spent most waking hours. I found myself walking back and forth, attempting to appear candid, as if I were only passing through. I would sometimes encounter another walker, most often out with a dog, taken for the need of shitting. Keeping this pretence of mine going, respectable before strangers should they pass me by, exhausted me more than the walking up and down. Not knowing for sure what Gordon intended by his throwing of books hardly helped my state of mind. As I rushed down to collect his books before rain and rot consumed them, I could not be entirely sure, as I had once been, that these books were intended for me. It was not guaranteed that Gordon threw out books for me to collect—carefully selected books, I had once presumed—or, alternatively, if they were the books he most despised, or had least use for. For why else did he discard some and walk on with others. But even useless books would instruct me, I decided. Useless books would reveal Gordon's thinking as if they were photographic negatives of his thought. Uncertain which it was—whether I was handling books that were of great significance, and were intended for me as such, or books that were of little or no significance to Gordon—I was unable to analyse their content, or spend any time reading them, and so come to a better understanding of Gordon. Besides, I could hardly spare the time to read what Gordon discarded. I was anxious to remain alert. I must collect Gordon's books first, I decided, prevent further decay, and then assemble them later to drive out their significance. My intellect was entirely absorbed in the collecting of books. It was completely understandable. I occupied myself with increasing my chances of getting to Gordon's books before they disintegrated. That, given the circumstances, seemed reasonable. My attempts to maintain some kind of front before other city dwellers, mainly dog walkers filling the undergrowth with shit, gradually gave way as I decided that this effort to look respectable decreased my efficiency. It reduced my chances of seeing Gordon well enough in advance to hide, and then get to his books in time. I allowed myself to appear ridiculous to these passers-by as I fingered through leaves and muck, all of whom must have wondered what kind of man this was, half starved, crouching at the edge of his path looking earnestly to the path below. None attempted to rescue me from that condition, as I feared they might, or commit me to some asylum or psychiatric ward. I knew my sanity would appear questionable to those who could not see my motives and understand the irrepressible logic of my actions. I was driven to neglect my appearance because of that logic. My shabby appearance was a pure and perfect expression of my commitment to the irrepressible logic of my actions. I was a reasonable being, I decided, a rational actor in the face of adversity. My outward appearance was a perfect manifestation of my inwardly logical nature. Eventually I stayed in place whole nights through, gathering some branches around me for warmth. Around that time the installation of new streetlights commenced along the upper edge of the hollow. These lights were installed right above the hollow where we walked, and I now crouched, just as they were installed elsewhere in the city. The entire city would soon have its lights replaced. They bristled with white light from their flawless light-emitting diodes, eyeballing me with relentless luminescence, and completely altered the conditions of my work. The quality of light was absolutely changed in my hollow. Amber light from the old sodium lamps was replaced with white light. The sodium lights no longer burned red and brightened into a mellow orange, a transition at dusk I had known and enjoyed since childhood. They came on immediately, these new lights, and shocked me every time flooding the hollow with their white light. It should have assisted me, the light, but only helped where the light was cast, and even there it was useless. Any shadow caused by a tree was much darker than before. The white lights entirely destroyed my ability to see in the gloom, in the hollow. They made an entire city, and a whole population, intolerant of darkness. Given a little white light, the city wished for more. An entire city hoped to bleach out its night, I thought, only deepening its shadows. Moonlit nights were completely useless to me now; they barely changed the conditions under which I worked. Clouded nights hardly made any difference. The orange glare of the city, which was reflected by low-lying clouds, had once lit my time in the hollow. That gentle glare—repellent in its own way—helped me as I moved about. It too, was gone. I could see nothing now that was not directly positioned under these new lights. Each time I looked up any vision I had gained since looking down was entirely destroyed. It was insufferable. The darkness was only more absolute as a result of these lights, I thought. It had become entirely black where the streetlights were intermittent, and was completely bleached out where they were in full glare. I was plunged into darkness by these lights. It was almost entirely pointless to stay here at night in the hollow. It was all either black or bleached out. Driven wild by these streetlights I constructed a shelter in which I sat blind and completely dejected. Or was it a small tree, or the upturned roots that became my shelter, as I sat completely done in by all this lamentable white light. At dawn I hardly noticed the arrival of daylight. I was still sitting lamenting the night, or the lack of it. I stowed Gordon's last books where I sat, driving them into a wedge between two roots. I was aware that the books in my shelter were rotting, that the rot was already set in when I picked them up. I could not spare the time it would take to bring them home and dry them, or decant them at my desk in the open-plan office. I had not visited the office for some time now. It could no longer be assumed that the desk I once occupied was still there for me. Somebody else sat doing nothing now, or something that amounted to nothing, or almost nothing, I thought. Occasionally I would glance through the books I assembled. I would allow myself to do so if Gordon had just passed by. If Gordon had just been seen, he was surely guaranteed or almost guaranteed not to return in the next few minutes. I was half blind. The light conditions had ruined my eyes. I could hardly think. I was succumbing to the rot myself, I thought, a type of intellectual rot from which I could no longer assemble Gordon's reading. Books that contained copious notes indicating Gordon's thinking were bled out and useless by the time I retrieved them. Some pages were stained more than others. Once that would have sufficed. Such pages would be given priority. Now I could not begin to construct his thought by looking at those pages. My devotion to Gordon was unmatched, I told myself. But I could no longer attempt to understand Gordon. The thought of Gordon no longer competed with the thought of work. The thought of work no longer hindered the study of Gordon. I had achieved a degree of separation from work that retirement would never allow. The university was already falling apart when I first met Gordon. But even a ruined institution can still grip you. The sector as a whole was already sliding into a hollow of its own making when I first saw him. Only the books Gordon threw away mattered, though they were falling apart in my hands. There was no escaping their fate. The preservation of these books for a future, less barbaric age, was out of the question. The preservation of books and the preservation of our ability to read and understand books no longer made sense to me. The rain was continuous. Not another, I thought, each time Gordon appeared with a book. I was sick with them. His books were either calculated to make me sick, or they made me sick anyway. I had become so wet with rain and sodden with books I could no longer stay even remotely dry. The days were as cold as the nights. I allowed myself to get so cold it gnawed at me. I was so tense and fatigued with cold that not even a brisk walk would raise my temperature let alone return feeling to my hands and feet. Only once before had I been this cold, allowing myself to remain still for so long and in such an uncomfortable state that my body reached a new level of insensate peace. It was a familiar, but forgotten resting place, this peace that sets in when the shivering stops, where thought, not even the thought of death, is impossible. It surprised me then, as it no longer did now, that it would take hours to recover, that it would be so painful, and that a recovery was by no means guaranteed. I had been still for too long. Gordon's visits had become occasional, and eventually rare. It hardly surprised me to discover Gordon was gone entirely and would never return. The last time Gordon passed by, several days ago, or weeks, he walked without a book, held no pen, and his hands were clean of ink. Gordon was almost unrecognisable without his book, his pen, and his ink-stained hands. Gordon approached, then turned, and took a different path, one that descended more rapidly into the hollow. I was entirely slow to respond as it became clear to me that Gordon would not return. No book, no pen, no ink, I kept repeating. Gordon's books were pure mulch. It took hours, days, for me to regain control of my limbs. Departing from this mass of rotting paper, I pitched myself down the bank, picked myself up, and staggered along his path, and then down my own, swinging legs that remained rigid. I had never considered taking Gordon's old route, but followed it now as it diverged from mine. On instinct I drove myself through parts of the city I hardly knew, slowly becoming aware of my steps before others. As I walked, I eventually found other wanderers, and similar encampments strewn across the metropolis, linking one wasteland to another, often lying close to schools and university departments and filled with rotting books of their own. Gordon walked, returning by this loop to the place from which he would depart. But that place, his workplace, was no longer there. As the wanderers confirmed, Gordon's loop no longer existed as paced by Gordon.

The Sick List
By Ansgar Allen

First published in this edition by Boiler House Press, 2021
Part of UEA Publishing Project
Copyright © Ansgar Allen, 2021

The right of Ansgar Allen to be identified as the Author of this
work has been asserted by him in accordance with the Copyright, Design & Patents Act, 1988.

Cover Design and Typesetting by Louise Aspinall
Typeset in Arnhem Pro
Printed by Tallinn Book Printers
Distributed by NBN International

ISBN: 978-1-911343-76-9